GRASS STAINS

Kirsty Robinson is the former editor and co-founder of the award-winning style magazine *Marmalade* and cult magazine *PiL*. She has written for various newspapers including the *Sunday Times*, *Independent on Sunday*, *Mail on Sunday* and *Guardian*. Born in Kent in 1972, she now lives in London with her husband and two young children.

KIRSTY ROBINSON

Grass Stains

Published by Vintage 2010

2 4 6 8 10 9 7 5 3 1

First published in Great Britain in 2010 by Vintage

Vintage
Random House, 20 Vauxhall Bridge Road,
London SW1V 2SA

www.vintage-books.co.uk

Addresses for companies within The Random House Group
Limited can be found at:
www.randomhouse.co.uk/offices.htm

The Random House Group Limited Reg. No. 954009

A CIP catalogue record for this book
is available from the British Library

ISBN 9780099541196

The Random House Group Limited supports The Forest Stewardship
Council (FSC), the leading international forest certification
organisation. All our titles that are printed on Greenpeace
approved FSC certified paper carry the FSC logo.
Our paper procurement policy can be found at
www.rbooks.co.uk/environment

Typeset in Adobe Caslon by Palimpsest Book Production Limited,
Grangemouth, Stirlingshire

Printed and bound in Great Britain by
CPI Cox & Wyman, Reading RG1 8EX

For Luke

One

I walk through the dark communal hallway, out of the front door into the sunshine that's hitting our terraced south London street, and put my hand through my hair. Fucking typical. I haven't rinsed the conditioner out properly. Combined with the familiar feeling that every single pore in my body is gently sweating booze, it's like I've been covered in a thin, greasy hung-over film for as long as I can remember.

I'm in pieces. Instead of leaving work and getting home to pack my bag for the weekend, I spent most of yesterday evening on the pavement outside a pub in Soho. Now, with the taste of last night's vodka still lurking at the back of my mouth and just about keeping a lid on the sparks of anxiety that might easily explode into a full-blown panic attack, my canvas holdall is jammed with half-dry clothes wrapped in supermarket carrier bags.

My nerves have been fizzing on and off since around five this morning when I woke dehydrated and immediately terrorised by the first thought that came into my head: I'd left my cash card behind the bar. I sprang out of bed, darted into the lounge holding my tits and emptied my handbag out onto the floorboards. The bank card was there along with my keys, train ticket, make-up bag, specks of tobacco, some drinks tokens for a party last week, three hairbands and a pair of knickers.

The knickers. Last night is a crudely edited memory. Less than twenty minutes after sneaking back to the office for a graceless, grubby fumble on the meeting-room table, I'm stumbling in red patent heels down Charing Cross Road and just manage to make the last train home. The train is packed with City blokes in bad suits eating Burger Kings, feeling up the office girls they've pulled. I sit there, looking down my nose, until I remember my knickers are in my handbag.

I've hit a new low: it's the first time in the six years I've been with Dan that I've done anything like it. Anything goes but this and for it to have been with the kind of guy who gets off with interns and goes to Coldplay gigs is bananas. Thank God I put the brakes on and got out the door before I shagged him.

Somehow, though, the relief that I'd managed to make it home with all my things, combined with a pint glass of water and some Nurofen, armed me with enough sense to pull the shutters and slouch back into bed for another couple of hours. I need as much help as I can get riding this one out, especially with so much at stake this weekend.

I woke again, the second time, with an image of my husband Dan and I framed by early-evening sunshine. We were at the top of a grassy hill. The sound of music and the hustle and bustle of people milling around came from the field below.

At around ten Dan called to let me know he was 'mangled' and that I could pick him up from his friend Tom's.

In the living room, next to yesterday's screwed-up jeans, my new red patent shoes are another casualty. Three hundred quid of shiny leather with chunks out of both heels and sludge on the bright white insoles. No time now to wipe them clean or patch them up. There's not even any time to get wound up with Dan for not making it home when he knows we need to hit the road first thing.

Instead I've been concentrating on pulling mental U-turns and avoiding the trains of thought that will have me curled back up on the sofa under a fake-fur throw staring at my reflection in the blank TV screen. In the same half-cocked, slapdash style that I've crammed my own weekend bag, I've filled up Dan's with a random mix of T-shirts, jeans, shorts and trainers

3

so that I can pick him up on the way out of town, get straight on the motorway and down to the festival.

The taste of melon-flavoured lip gloss mingles with the stale alcohol in my mouth as I reach into my bag and fish around for car keys. I wish I'd snorted the line of coke I'd been offered earlier in the evening by Cherry, the receptionist at the magazine where we all work, and sharpened up. I'd have gladly traded the comedown for the bile-churning memory of that senseless grope in the office, but I held back because I was getting up early in the morning for a weekend away with Dan.

The car, an old red Golf I've had for even longer than I've been with my husband, is looking shoddier than normal. The windscreen's covered with sticky splodges of sap from the tree that stands directly outside the flat, and in the sunlight the matt patch of paint-work on the bonnet is even more noticeable, offering nothing to reflect from.

Inside, after I turn the key in the ignition, I tilt my neck and check myself in the rear-view mirror, nonplussed at what I see. My roots are coming through and my long dirty-blonde hair is on the cusp of becoming two-tone.

I'm paranoid about looking cheap and the kind of work I do makes me worse. I'm the features editor at *Neon*, an edgy, agenda-setting style magazine, and I'm also the office misfit: get past the smattering of designer labels, Topshop bargains and second-hand finds and there is nothing particularly 'fashion' about me. I didn't go to art school. I don't have bohemian middle-class parents, a foreign-sounding name or several generations' worth of vintage 'pieces' to fall back on when I'm stuck for something to wear to a party. I was brought up in a fifties bungalow in a village on the rural outskirts of a tatty Thames Estuary town and was the first person in my family to go to university.

I pull at my eyes. The dark circles under them seem worse when my hair gets like this. I stare down at the hair and fluff that's collected around the base of the gearstick, wrinkle my forehead, gripped again by a lurching feeling of despair. Pain-in-the-arse mood swings. Deep breaths. I let the mid-morning sun that's coming through the windscreen fill me up. I'm getting out of town. Gently rushing with a familiar mix of excitement, nerves and impatience, I take out a CD from the glove compartment, whack the music up, nod my head and pull off.

Within a few hours I'll be in the middle of the countryside, sipping beer from a plastic cup, and wearing a laminated pass and fluorescent wristband.

The cul-de-sac where our friends Tom and Zoë live is still and quiet. The row of houses that line the pedestrian walkway leading away from the road's end have a muffling effect on the noise from the busy main road to the front. It's mostly old people who live here. Tom and Zoë's is the only place with blinds, the rest net curtains. I step out of the car, relieved that the sole of my foot can have a break from the clutch, but have no intention of going over to the house. I know they've been up all night and can guarantee the place will be littered with strung-out faces. To turn up, midday, comparatively fresh from a night in my own bed to drag Dan away would jar with the gang lolloping around behind those blinds. Instead I dial his mobile.

Twice it rings through to voicemail. The second time I leave a message. I stare at the front door, willing for it to swing open and spit Dan out, squinting, onto the pavement. The minutes drag by. I can feel tears start to burn in the corners of my eyes as I come to terms with walking over and ringing the bell. I'm still trying to squish down the feelings of panic that had been darting around my body since I'd first woken this morning. I can't face a house full of wired people. Finger pressed on the bell, I wait for Zoë to pull open the door, rollie in hand, wearing last night's strappy top and tracksuit bottoms. Instead, a short, fat guy with huge eyebrows is standing in front of me, in Tom's old Inspiral Carpets Mad As Fuck T-shirt. 'I've come to pick up Dan. Can you tell him I'm outside in the car?' I say in my work voice.

'He's not here. They went down the Mason's half an hour ago. Do you want me to give him a message?' he says, monotone.

'For fuck's sake. I'll go and pick him up from there.'

The Mason's Arms is less than five minutes away. It stagnates with the smell of spilt Stella and fags. The landlord is a crook and hard-faced middle-aged men in Reeboks and caps sell speed in the loos. Coming down in the Mason's could be construed as an act of self-punishment but, equally, because the place is so awful, it can sometimes make you hate yourself less. Collecting Dan from here today is even worse than it would have been from the house.

I scan the bar and see Zoë's bum in the air as she falls off her stool, her tiny body juddering, face bright red with laughter as she lies on her back on the burgundy beer-soaked carpet. Tom holds his head in his hands before staggering up to help his girlfriend back to her seat. They both straighten up the odd mix of jeans and T-shirts guaranteed to have been pulled on moments before leaving the house as a gesture to the new day and Tom nods an apology to the landlord. By now I've reached the table, standing awkwardly, hands in my back pockets. The smell of booze makes me purse my lips but I squeeze out a smile. Everyone is turned towards me, all crooked grins, porous skin and eye bogeys.

Dan is sat on a bench, legs crossed, smoking, wearing a wife-beater, jeans and sunglasses. The crow's feet at the corner of his eyes fan out from each side of his shades. He's wedged between Gareth, one of Tom's friends from back home, and a girl I don't know: she's pretty, thinner than me, but her top's cheap, shiny and synthetic.

The girl smiles but not before a wave of disappointment at my arrival fleets across her face. I look straight through her, even though her forearm is touching Dan's. It takes everything I've got to remain composed and contain any clues to the guilt that's been jutting around my mind.

Dan takes his sunglasses off and, after feeling so nervy, I'm relieved to lock eyes with him. He's fucked. He doesn't have a clue. Even if he weren't so out of it, the thought wouldn't cross his mind.

My husband's light green eyes are tired but laughing. It's a welcome alternative to the thunderous stare I'm sometimes met with after he's been out on a bender.

'Hey, babes, I was just going to call you, let you know we're down the road,' says Dan, raising his eyebrows at me as if it were Sunday afternoon and they'd all decided to go for a pint after lunch. 'Fancy a quick one before we shoot?' he asks, looking down at his half-filled glass, patting his lap inviting me to sit down.

It's been bad enough having to come in here; the

thought of having to make small talk with this lot, in the state they're in, gives me the fear. With Dan on an up I try to sound chirpy, reasonable, mouth to Zoë that she has tobacco in her teeth, but I'm looking to get the hell out the door and back into the car. 'You know what? I'll give it a miss. We're running so late already. We need to get down the motorway, I've arranged to meet people . . . Sorry.'

'Just one?'

Dan was at it again, making me look like a party-pooper. I pull my trump card, the only thing that will get him out of this ropey old boozer.

'Do you want a backstage pass or not? I told Ramona we'd be there by five.'

Sure enough Dan tilts his head back, widens his mouth and sinks his beer. The only reason my husband leaves a party is for a better one.

TWO

The warm heavy air inside the car sticks to my skin and I watch the tiny beads of sweat around Dan's hairline swell as he climbs into the passenger seat. Straight away he pulls down the visor in front, checks himself and wipes both corners of his mouth. Out in the sunlight the vintage gold-framed Aviator sunglasses I bought as a birthday present are his saving grace.

Catching my eye, he gets it all wrong, leans over and puts his clammy hand on the inside of my thigh. I'm paralysed by the smell of stale smoke, sweat and coke-stoked pheromones. Dan backs off. Realising he's mistaken, he reaches behind, pulls out a beer from a bag on the back seat and retreats to the stereo, replacing Jack White with a folky girl doing a lazy cover of 'All Shook Up'. Neither of us says anything.

The beer, strumming guitars and honey-voiced girl

11

soon sedate him, and within minutes of reaching the motorway Dan seems hypnotised by road signs showing airport symbols, Costa Coffee logos and arrows to Chessington World of Adventures. It's a relief he's in the car. Next to me but miles away.

The thing about Dan that got me hooked is the thing about him that also does my head in. He's a grizzly mix of stubble, cheekbones, fuck-you unpredictability and occasional effeminate gestures. Rounded off with a knack for sweating testosterone after a few drinks.

Everyone's bowled over by his swagger at first, and the way that it's underpinned by a suggestion of a gentler sensuality is something else. Gay men love the paradox, and the straight ones, they can't get enough of him because at the end of the day he'll always go that extra mile, neck that extra pill, fuck work, take a taxi. If there's a line to cross he'll walk on his hands over it.

When we first met, simply the idea of him made me prickle with excitement, and as we tore around town through the night, I would shake my head in disbelief at the way he lived up to his hype, then smile that this man was my very own grown-up boyfriend. There was a momentum to our adventure, a velocity that was instantly addictive. Each time we bowled through another door then down another set of stairs into another noisy, smoke-filled room, the whole thing became even bigger, even better than the night before. In turn that shaped everything that followed.

Now I'm finally growing up a bit, it's verging on embarrassing to think that he reeled me in with his no-brakes, head-on, fuck-everything manifesto. To think how, in the beginning, I even loved pulling off his grimy jeans and sweat-soaked sneakers, tucking him into bed and stroking the raised veins on his forehead when he resurfaced, broken, after disappearing for a day or two. But this was what we did, how we lived, and I loved it. If there were medals for valiant services to fuckyourselfupdom, my husband would have a chestful, and I was his proud and supportive wife.

In fairness it wasn't just hedonistic charisma that I fell for. Even though Dan hasn't ever been big on his career and he's the kind of guy he is, he does have a bent for more contained thoughtfulness: I'd be at work, couldn't get hold of him and instantly assume that he was writing the day off in the pub. Then I'd come home to find a pile of old yellow paperbacks that he'd bagged after an afternoon spent browsing in the row of musty second-hand bookshops in town. Every so often I would stumble upon curveball pockets of calm in his life and it was like walking into the hairdresser's to find the stereo tuned to Radio 3.

They might seem thin on the ground now but during that first phase of intense clubbing and shagging Dan managed to squeeze in a flurry of charming little episodes, exposing much more than his hedonistic battle armour suggested. He turned up outside a club in the early hours with a big coat for me to wear home when the winter nights started to kick in, surprised me with a weekend on a friend of his family's houseboat in Marlow and danced with my nan all night at a cousin's wedding. Dan can be sweet, thoughtful and kind too.

The bummer is that his soaring fearlessness, the appetite for adventure that pulled us together so powerfully, is in danger of eclipsing all of the other good stuff as it snowballs into recklessness and don't-carelessness.

His job at the restaurant is hanging by a thread. A few weeks back he blurted down the phone that he'd got into trouble – he wouldn't say what, just 'trouble' – and was seven hundred pounds down in the till. It was a week away from payday but I scraped the money together and headed down there to give it to him. I didn't want to condone whatever it was he'd done, but Dan losing his job – even if it's one he can't stand – is the last thing we need. He's been so up and down in the last few months. Suddenly becoming unemployed would be a disaster.

By the time I arrived, Dan's specky deputy Simon had clocked what was going on and confronted him. True to form, Dan soon buttered Simon up and bought himself some time: Simon agreed to hold off from squealing to the area manager so long as the money got back to where it should be.

I don't like the place. It's a worn-out branch of a middle-of-the-road Tex-Mex chain, but I thought Dan could do with some company so I stuck around. We hung out in the back office with a couple of bottles of house wine surrounded by rotas, photos of the Sri Lankan kitchen staff at the Christmas party, and health and safety notices. I sat gripping my glass, layering it with smears, watching Dan put away line after line. After the last waiter had said his goodbyes we went out front and sat by the bar with the lights dimmed.

We'd been chatting away, I can't remember exactly what I said, something about how he hadn't been himself recently and maybe it'd be worth making an appointment at the doctor's, when he flipped. Dan stormed round behind the bar. One by one, he threw bottle after bottle out into the restaurant, before sweeping his arm along a shelf filled with glasses, sending them crashing onto the tiles. As I stared at the spiky cocktail of Kahlúa, vodka, gin, whisky and crème de menthe that covered the floor, I felt something cold dripping onto my forehead. Dan had saved the Baileys for me. He tipped the whole lot on my head and lobbed the empty bottle straight into one of the enormous mirrors at the back of the place.

Even in the shattered glass I recognised the subtle shift in his eyes when he morphs from the man I married – someone who regularly spends over an hour shopping for the ingredients required to make the perfect cheese and ham sandwich (Quicke's Farm Cheddar, ham sliced at local grocer, crusty white loaf) – into a disconnected shell.

I don't remember getting home. The shutters came down. Next morning I woke alone, hair like cardboard. I found Dan in the lounge twisted with insomnia, Jack Daniel's and whatever the drugs on the coffee table were still cooking up for him.

I called Simon to forewarn him about what he'd find when he opened up in a few hours' time, begged him to cut Dan some slack, give us some time to get him straightened out. By now Dan was on the floor, sobbing, pleading with me to help him.

He hasn't made an appointment at the doctor's yet but Dan does have his official disciplinary with his area manager next week.

For a few hours in this crappy old car, though, we're nowhere near the kind of people we've been spending more and more time with lately. People who are so disappointed and uninspired by their lives that they'd rather call in sick and hide behind the curtains than go to work, see their families or bother to turn up to meet their friends.

This weekend is going to be different. We'll have a few drinks, steer clear of the all-nighters, dick around in the sunshine and, maybe, it will be the thing that turns the corner for us.

I'm thirty-one this year. There's a lot of bullshit spouted about women my age refusing to disrupt their fabulous lives with serious relationships, but I've never pretended that I love living on my own. I'm from an old-school, happily married family. Dan as well – his parents down on the south coast are always going to golf-club dinner dances and off on weekends away, even now – and although it might be at odds with the rest of our lives, there's something inherently traditional, unfashionably conventional, about both of us in that way.

Maybe this weekend I'll start to get back some more of the man I married. Someone that loves *Saturday Kitchen*, old house music and graphic novels. A man who can be as thoughtful as he is full on. Someone who brings me the papers and a takeaway curry in bed on a Sunday evening when I've been hung-over and unable to move all day. The guy everyone wants at the party.

By the time we get to the Welcome Break my bum's stuck to my seat. We stop next to a man in a short-sleeved shirt and suit trousers, standing by his Audi saloon, talking into his phone, beaming smile. Windows wound right down I can hear him chatting to his kid, asking how school was and if they're looking forward to the cinema.

The car door slams shut and I see Dan leg it across the car park. I lean out of the window and yell at him to meet me outside the loos, but a van pulls in front, blocking my view. As I pick up my purse and pull myself out of the shabby VW, the monoxide breeze that is coming off the carriageway scratches against the back of my throat.

I look up to see a pale, lanky guy in a top hat, suit jacket, drainpipes and pointy brogues unfolding out from the side of the van in front. He's followed by three more cocky, long-haired variations on the theme. They squint, drag on cigarettes and look around like they're making a pit stop in the desert. Either they're a two-bit band on the way to the festival or they want to be. A couple of girls appear. One is tall and skinny with glossy, dark brown shoulder-length hair in a fifties halter-neck dress with a cute little handbag. The other is rougher, shorter, stockier; all bleached-blonde hair, sunglasses, black lycra and knee-high boots. I'm sweating even more just looking at her.

I make my way through the Welcome Break, contemplating a sugary bottle of Dr Pepper after a quick wee and a change into some shorts. Goosebumpy from the air con, I walk past a tracksuit-clad family huddled round a fruit machine; four pasty working-class faces illuminated by flashing lights.

There's not much of a queue in the Ladies and I grab a cubicle towards the end. Plonking myself down on the seat I look down at my battered Converse, lift my feet up onto my toes. There's a break in the drone of the hand dryers lining the wall just outside. I'm full flow, weeing straight onto the water. Embarrassed by the noise, I spread my weight further towards the front of the seat and aim at the porcelain. A few minutes later, I'm still sitting there, elbows on knees, chin in my hands, staring blankly at a sticker bearing the logo and telephone number of a pregnancy advice service, feeling vaguely sad about nothing in particular.

My ears prick up and my attention is refocused on two women moaning about their musician boyfriends just the other side of the door. It's the girls I saw outside with the band. I pull off my shoes and jeans as quickly as I can, straining to listen in. The tall one, she had to be a model. I yank my denim shorts on, and pushing my feet inside my shoes like they're slippers with the backs trodden down, I open the door. Up close, next to the two of them, in front of the basins and mirrors, I'm juggling uninterest with enough sideways glances to build a picture. I lean forward into the mirror, study my eyebrows carefully then reach for the tweezers in my make-up bag on the counter, pull at a couple of stray hairs and wonder if there's any mileage in a muso spin-off of *Trisha* for MTV.

Rather than loiter directly outside the toilets I head over to the newsagent's for a flick through this week's *Heat*. It must be ten minutes since I've been out here. What's Dan up to now? Walking over to the sliding doors at the entrance, I shield my eyes from the sun with my right hand and look for signs of him by the car. The space where the van had stood is now filled by a Mini. I see my worn-out red car easily, but no Dan.

His phone rings a few times before going to voice-mail. What could he be doing halfway down a fucking motorway? In just quarter of an hour, it's looking like Dan's done one of his disappearing acts and now the place is absolutely teeming with people. Stay calm, be practical. I haven't eaten since yesterday afternoon, so I go back into the newsagent's and pick up a ploughman's sandwich from the chilled cabinet and a bag of Hula Hoops. By the time I'm paying at the till, my stomach's turning. Please, not already, Dan. I shove the carrier bag in my holdall, pull out a packet of Marlboro Menthols and head outside.

As soon as I light the cigarette, my stomach lurches again. I don't smoke normally unless I have a drink. My head's swimming with nicotine and my insides are churning. I try the mobile again. This time it goes straight to voicemail.

The second I hang up, the handset vibrates and the drama's over. Dan must have been calling me at the same time. If only. The incoming call is from Alexa, my editor, the last person I need to talk to right now. I stare at the flashing screen helplessly for a few seconds before picking up, intimidated already with thoughts of her ugly, edgy fashion and west London sense of entitlement.

'Alexa. Hi.'

'Hi, Louisa. What's happening?' I immediately recognise the over-friendly tones my boss is using as those most editors employ when mollycoddling fuck-up writers into delivering the goods. First-day web coverage of the festival is due and I'm not even on-site.

I imagine her pacing around the office, smiling through clenched teeth, in one of her outfits. I can't bear her, the fact that she's three years younger than me or the way she uses the magazine as a vehicle to promote herself.

'Louisa, are you OK? I started to get worried when we hadn't heard from you. Maybe you'd had a terrible prang in the car or something.'

The nicer she gets, the more fucked off she is. I know. I do the same thing with people myself when they flake on me.

'Alexa, the roads are totally jammed. I'll be another hour at most and then I'll get the first piece over straight away.'

Her voice is verging on sing-song nice. My work has been incredibly hit-and-miss lately and this weekend is massive for the magazine. She must be furious. 'Tell you what, how about this? I pass the web stuff to that freelance kid Paul Vincent. He's been there since this morning and can knock something together quickly right now. You can save yourself for the big interview tomorrow. I'll see you afterwards – I'll be down by then too.'

The line goes dead. Alexa had hung up before I had a chance to say goodbye. I have to find Dan.

The automatic doors are as jumpy as I am. A few more carloads jammed with people, rucksacks and cases of beer have arrived. I wonder if I look like my husband's dumped me at the services and hitched a lift with someone more exciting. I see a guy on his own walking towards me; he looks familiar but I can't quite place him. He smiles at me as he talks into his phone and I smile back but as soon as I do I remember that I haven't fake-tanned my legs so I look away and rummage in my bag so he doesn't stop.

It's been twenty minutes now. I head back inside and scout around, pissed off. The vitamin-deficient track-suit family are still playing the fruitie. Dan's nowhere to be seen. I let my mind wander. He hasn't collapsed in the Gents; someone would have called an ambulance by now. I've a nagging suspicion that he might have gone for a wank after I'd given him the brush-off earlier. I let out a deep sigh, pull the cheese sandwich out of my bag and stare at the entrance to the Gents. At least he'll stop pestering me.

'Louisa, where've you been?'

I turn round, mouth stuffed with bread, cheese and pickle. Dan's standing behind me holding a bag full of beer, smiling. The nondescript carbs are a bit like Valium and I'm stuck for words. 'Here,' I mumble. 'And out there,' I say, pointing at the doors.

'Are you all right? You seem spaced out, babes. I just bumped into Camden Rob over by the lorries – Pete's down there already. What? Don't roll your eyes. No one said they were coming.'

'Fuck's sake ... What were you doing in the lorry park?'

'Looking for you, you daft bitch. Duh ...'

'Why would I be there?'

'I don't know. You weren't here.'

We start to walk outside and over to the car. I don't believe a single word my husband says.

Three

A makeshift sign by the road outside a farmhouse reads 'Last Shop Before Festival' and Dan shuffles around in his seat, looking for more clues in the fields either side. Sure enough, within about thirty seconds, yellow plastic cones line the edges of the lane and a shirtless, sunburnt refugee wanders disorientated, clutching a plastic Evian bottle filled with dark piss-coloured cider.

Soon we join a short queue of traffic that disappears over a gentle hump and I'm able to look more closely at the leaves that are brushing against the side of the car. The distant thud of sound systems gets louder as we roll slowly onwards. Dan stretches his arm round behind me and cups my head with his hand, gently pulling against the back of my hair. I turn, run the tips of my fingers across the side of his face and we both smile. Small smiles brought to an end by the sound of the horn from the car behind us.

A fat woman wearing a fluoro tabard and combats waves me past what must be the main entrance to the site, towards the car park, but a couple of crusties step out in front of us just as I move off. One of them is pushing a battered-up old bike, the other pulling along a trailer with some speakers. I brake and the second the seat belts relax again Dan stretches out of his window.

'Get out of the fucking way . . .'

They carry on walking, deliberately slower. I can see the colour rush back into Dan's grey face.

Thankfully the two guys, bike and trailer disappear into the main entrance. We dart along a short stretch of road and pull into the car park. I'm not sure how big a football pitch is but it must be the size of at least a couple. We stop and start, dodging men in England shirts and a small group of girls dressed as fairies until a beefy bloke with a tash orders us into a spot next to an enormous black shiny Porsche 4 x 4.

Before I've pulled the keys from the ignition Dan is out, pacing around on his phone, leaving the passenger footwell littered with empty cans and fag packets. I let it go and gather my purse, phone and hoodie.

I look up to see two familiar faces coming towards us laughing, shaking their heads, looking like trouble.

Straight away I feel defensive and disappointed. Get either on their own and you can have a civilised conversation but together Gucci Steve and Al are a pair of charmless City boys. Flash and crass, they idolise Dan, aping and magnifying his largesse with their extravagance, persistently egging each other on. The three of them bring out the most extreme versions of themselves and the mirror they hold up to each other legitimises the way they increasingly overstep the mark.

Steve is short, overweight and has no pubic hair. We once coincidentally spent a few days in the same enormous stuffy hotel in the south of France, both on work trips. We were strangers in town so I was a little warmer with him than normal and we met for a drink. After a few cocktails around the hotel-pool bar, Steve got the drugs out and lost the plot. Without uttering so much as a single word of warning he jumped up and somersaulted into the pool, still in his suit, in front of an audience of over a hundred people. I ran, dragged him out from the side and hurried him to my room to get dry. The door was barely shut when he'd stripped off, naked bar his Patek Philippe watch. Then the crazy fucker started doing that hip-swinging thing that little boys do to make their willies bounce around, dancing and giggling. I threw a robe at him and pushed him back into the corridor. Gucci Steve is completely bald.

I don't have any funny Alistair stories. On the surface

he's a softly spoken, Prada-smart, ex-public-school boy from a nice family in Wiltshire but simmering beneath is a man with serious women issues. Like Steve, Al rarely has a regular girlfriend around but the last time he did the relationship crashed to a dramatic end with a series of explosive rows and rumours of neighbours calling the police. Something about him makes my skin crawl.

'Danny boy, what's happening?' Gucci Steve is all smiles and hand-rubbing as he stops in front of the car. Al's a little more sedate, nodding hello. Both look at me briefly, out of courtesy to Dan and the chance I might have extra backstage passes.

'Nice one, lads. Don't know how the fuck we made it down here. It got really fucking messy around Tom's last night,' brags Dan, legs wide apart, arms crossed, head nodding.

'I know, you turkey. You spoke to me. Just as well I didn't drive over cos all I've got is what we'd lined up earlier in the week.'

Dan laughs shallowly, feeling my eyes burning into him. He'd known they were going to be down here for days and had organised to hook up but hadn't said a dicky bird to me. He'd let me carry on thinking this was going to be a proper weekend away. What a sucker.

'What zone's your camping pass?' pipes up Alistair, feeling the tension and attempting to diffuse it.

'We don't have a zone,' I say, pouncing on the

opportunity to put some distance between us. 'Work's got me a tent in the boutique field, away from the main part.'

'So why don't we meet up later? We're off down the road,' says Steve, making a big deal that they're up to something.

'Bell you in a bit. Come on, Lou, let's get our shit together.'

I watch until Gucci Steve and Al are out of earshot. 'You've arranged to spend the weekend with them, haven't you?'

'They asked if we were going to be here. What could I say?'

'There's no fucking way we're spending the weekend with those two. If they call you, ignore it.'

'Calm down, Lou, stop being a headcase. We won't meet them.'

'You're a complete arsehole, Dan.' They turn up and I just fade into the background, pick up the pieces when it goes tits up. 'There's no way you're meeting up with them.'

'Shut the fuck up, Louisa. I've said I'm not going to – I'm here with you, so just drop it. I called and told you where I was this morning, didn't I? The others were off to Brixton to carry on drinking but I wanted to come here, with you. Stop telling me what I should and shouldn't do. OK?' Dan looks right into my eyes, puts both hands on my shoulders and smiles. 'I said OK, you daft cow.'

'OK . . . Have you got any money left after last night?'

Dan looks at me but says nothing. No then. My heart sinks at how pathetic he can be but I don't like the idea of people we know thinking he hasn't got any money in his pocket to buy a round of drinks. So I give him fifty quid.

'I'll give you some cash next week, Lou. Promise.'

With just a couple of bags and some booze, the walk over to the entrance should be light work, but without any shade, the heat continues to bear down on us. Early evening and there's still no let-up.

'Where are the tickets?'

'In my bag, but we've got to trade them for wristbands somewhere. Probably over there.'

We both look at a row of Portakabins mobbed with people, separated into herds by crash barriers. I plonk my bag on the dirt track by the side of the road into the site and step back a few paces while a massive blacked-out tour bus passes, throwing up dust and tiny pieces of grit.

'No way, they've given me one press ticket, the other's only a regular one, Dan, without any access to the VIP bars . . . Look, it's not a problem, Ramona has that backstage pass for you which means you can go anywhere – we'll just have to find her straight away.'

'Whatever. Let's get in there.'

I strain my eyes at the signs above each window of the line of Portakabins and Dan plants a kiss on my forehead.

'That queue, second in on the left, is shortest for normal collections. I've got to go over to the other end. See you in a bit.'

Ten minutes later and the line for regular tickets is moving nowhere fast. A troop of leggy, long-haired sixth-form indie girls bounce around me as I excuse my way through, peering over shoulders for signs of Dan's crew cut and white vest. All around me people are gazumping each other with festival stories. It reminds me of a fortnight in Goa, with gap-year kids in every beach bar talking about how much better it is in Kerala. I push my way right through to the front, turn round, stand on my tiptoes, tilt my neck back. Head down, I push back through.

Dan's nowhere to be seen and his phone's straight to voicemail as usual. There's no way he could have got his wristband before me. I give my husband the benefit of the doubt but as the minutes dissolve one after the other and the first gentle gushes of cool early-evening breeze pull things down a notch or two, my breath quickens and the tears start burning at the corner of my eyes for the second time today. I can feel it in my gut. This time he really has split.

Hands pushed deep into my shorts' pocket, frozen to the spot, I watch a couple of fat tears drop onto my dusty Converse. I wipe my nose, sniff, wondering if I'm a bit past it as the sixth-formers' legs trot by.

I'd been feeling so pleased with myself. I'd managed to get Dan out of the pub, prise him away from Steve and Alistair and he was in fairly good shape. With a few quid back in his pocket though, he'd sniffed out another route in, probably with those two twats, and dropped me. Again.

The clock on my phone says it's almost seven thirty. Dan's shiny stoned face moons out at me. I really need to change my screen saver. A part of me feels like jumping straight back in the car and heading off back home, but I've got work to do and a wedding to go to here as well.

I know people must wonder what on earth I'm doing with him, but it wasn't always like this. Before Dan started behaving like a delinquent teenager, we were a tight little unit, out and about every night. We lapped up the parties and perks that come with my job together in one long, happy, loved-up haze. I genuinely thought coming down here on our own might get a bit of that back.

We used to do silly, dumb stuff. Like slipping into my office after last orders, pilfering vodka that had been sent in by some drinks company or other and rifling through the fashion cupboard. Ten minutes later we'd be up the top on the number 55 on the way to a party, swigging from bottles, wearing daft outfits.

However the night started and whatever we were wearing, we'd invariably finish it off by wandering around the East End, freezing our nuts off at dawn, looking for a ride home. Once we'd found a magic tree-scented minicab prepared to go south of the river, we'd sit holding hands, watching people starting to make their way to work. Coming down, we'd agree to phone in sick for each other and spend the day in bed.

People don't turn into arseholes overnight. For the life of me, I can't put my finger on when it happened to Dan.

After a big row, while the dust settles, we invariably dissect his frustrations at work. I say it's him and not a six-figure salary I married. He says he desperately wants to do something more creative and over the past year or so I've seen his self-esteem, the guts of the man, ebb away.

Dan's always been a face around town and, until we got married and he got the job at the restaurant, he hopped about, doing this and that. Which is great in your twenties, but now his eroding thirty-two-year-old male ego can't hack that he's missed the boat with the sort of career he never got round to carving out for himself. Rather than dig his heels in and turn things around, this charismatic man, who never gave a toss about doing things by the book, is increasingly defeated. Once proud of my progress at work, he's frequently irritated at even the mention of it. Now when he's my plus one at a party he downs four or five drinks and then fucks off somewhere else on his own.

There's a tipping point at which the floods of tears become a tiny trickle. No matter how much I want things to get back to how they were, there's only so many times I can muster up the energy to sob over someone who does a runner when we go out together.

Why am I standing here like a lemon? The guys from work will be inside, along with thousands and thousands of others. If Dan wants to play silly buggers, let him. I'll find him later.

I pick up my bags and start walking in time to some music coming from a site van rolling along beside me. In the space of a couple of minutes, I'm through a turnstile and halfway down a steep hill headed in the direction of the main stage.

I cast my eyes over the dusty, stoned alter egos of a stream of people I decide are a mix of call-centre workers, English teachers, off-duty policemen and fifteen-year-olds from the sticks. The balmy smoke-tinged evening air carries a muffled mix of music, broken every now and again into something more recognisable. I look down and the grass is the colour of school holidays; out in front on the opposite hill is a multicoloured tent town.

Out of the dusk comes a familiar voice from the direction of an organic burger van to the right. 'Oi, Lou!'

It's my friend Bart. I feel my whole body break into a smile, relieved that I've been rescued from my own inevitable half-cocked intellectualising about Roman Saturnalia and liminal zones. He's been working hard on new material for his band and we've not seen each other for over a month, but it doesn't matter, we're tight.

Big brown eyes and skinny-arse boy-in-a-band handsome, he's the one I call when my husband's been pacing around the flat after a massive bender and I've spent half an hour hiding under coats at the bottom of the wardrobe hoping he goes back out again.

Sinking his teeth into a big fat burger he takes a massive bite. 'I thought you might be down here. They're all crawling out of the woodwork.'

It sounds like half of London has relocated for the weekend.

'Let's have a bite.' I take two and pass it back.

We hug, both chewing. Bart has ketchup all the way down his T-shirt. 'I've had a shit time. Dan vanished when we were collecting our tickets. He's switched his phone off so I've got no idea what he's doing . . . Sorry, I'm really stinky.'

Bart looks at me, sniffs, shakes his head. He's only twenty-four and thinks I'm ancient. Somehow, in spite of a reputation for childish pratting around, he's also the king of sort-your-life-out honesty. 'What you talking about? You know exactly what he's doing. What he always does. Stupid husband. He's off with his mates, cramming as much coke up his stupid nose as he flaming well can.'

'I feel like such an idiot.'

'You *are* an idiot. If he pisses off the minute you arrive on holiday what do you expect he's gonna do here? Come on, where you going? I've left Helena and the others at the Total Relapse stage. Wander back there with me. You won't believe some of the states here.'

'What about my bags?'

Bart's not taking any bullshit whining. He takes one of my bags from me, starts walking. I make myself stop scanning the waves of sunburnt faces around us for Dan. I'm bemused to see for the first time in over ten years a group of girls who used to be in my class at school wearing versions of our old bottle-green uniform. They'd just come out of a tent with a 'School Days' sign at the entrance. I'm about to make a smart comment to Bart and decide not to. They look like they're having fun. I should keep my mouth shut for once.

Four

Desperately Seeking Susan pulled me in, hook, line and sinker, as a kid, and one scene especially bore a disproportionately deep etching onto my adolescent brain. From the seat of the local ABC cinema I sat glued to Madonna skanking around a New York nightclub packed with punked-up weirdos, industrial fittings and dry ice. 'Into the Groove' was playing and I couldn't imagine anyone in the club having parents. From then on, this was how I visualised all nightclubs and the people in them to be. Instantly and childishly seduced, my imagination ran wild and I started scrunching my hair.

I would have been about thirteen, living in Thatcher-voting nowheresville just off the M25. It may have been just forty minutes away from wherever it was in the West End that Boy George first started dancing in a dress, but the view from my bedroom's dormer window was unedifying. In one direction, a few miles beyond the farmer's fields at the back of our house, cars sped along the motorway to a huge interchange; in the other, a row of cement works' chimneys lining the edge of the Thames stood decaying, puffing away like dying old men resigned to a fatal prognosis.

I'd gone to see the film with my best friend Amy. She lived two roads away and we were both in the same swimming team. Only school kept us apart: I went to the all girls' grammar and Amy the mixed C of E comp.

We met the summer before secondary school in the midst of a minor coincidence: my family upgraded from town to the first bit of countryside on the way out and she started training at my swimming club because her dad had got to thinking that the coach at her old one wasn't up to the job. As soon as our parents realised we lived practically next door they organised a car rota to get us to and from the pool.

She was the only person I knew with a rat's tail, and while the other girls in my class ping-ponged between each other's houses, watching videos of *Grease* until the tape heads wore out, I hung out with Amy.

Forging the friendship that shapes your growing up, finding the best friend who is at the bedrock of what you're about, can be a bit like falling in love. Part chemical, part happy accident. We bought the same outfits, just in different colours, watched *Top of the Pops* and *EastEnders* together on the phone, and religiously flicked through *The Face* and *i-D* in Smith's, even though neither of us had a clue what they were really about.

Dark and dingy nightclubs didn't come until much later. We made do instead with under-18s civic-centre discos, where throughout the summer of *Susan* I wore a lace bow in my yellow Sun-Inned perm and Amy covered her forearms with cuffs and bangles.

It was the last Friday in September and the evenings were beginning to draw in. It had become much easier to knock about outside the town hall with our booze and fags without getting spotted by any parents doing drop-offs. Clusters of kids were twitching and poking around, charged with scratchy teenage energy. Inside, the red foyer carpet was littered with freshly discarded chewing gum and the sound of the Fatback Band was beckoning from the main hall.

Nothing much happened until Shelley, one of the girls from Amy's class, ran off to be sick. By the time we caught up with her in the loos another girl Lisa was bent down beside her, trying to keep her hair away from the puke she was depositing in the basin.

Amy and I stood there holding our noses, biting the insides of our cheeks, until the main door to the toilets flew open and Julie Barker, the fifteen-year-old town headcase, barged in. I'd only ever seen her from a distance before but I knew she had fights with boys, the police came and people went to hospital for stitches. She'd got a shiny jet-black bob, a sovereign on a chain around her neck and was wearing big baggy jeans. An intimidating amalgam of big boobs, Boots 17 Twilight Teaser lipstick and Elizabeth Duke jewellery.

'Stop pissing about, Lotta. Skin up.'

Julie looked across at us. 'Got a problem?'

Lotta had a big highlighted ponytail and gold-hooped earrings. She was Julie Barker's sidekick. They didn't seem like especially good friends. Behind them was Julie's cousin Clare. I played netball with her at primary school but I didn't think she could see past Lotta to where I was standing.

We shrugged our shoulders. None of us smoked weed, only boys smoked weed, but of course we didn't mind. Shelley shook her head, which was still over the basin.

Lotta and Julie swore constantly through clenched teeth as they fiddled around with fag papers and tobacco. Clare looked really bored when they started talking about bongs.

We were stuck. Leaving would have meant asking them all to move and Julie Barker famously started on people just for being there, so we kept quiet and waited. I looked at the scabs on Julie's knuckles then back down at Shelley's pink-and-beige sick. We all did. I kept my fingers crossed that after a gap of a couple of years Clare didn't twig that it was me there.

'Louisa?'

She must have been constantly on the lookout for anyone she might have been able to make normal thirteen-year-old-girl conversation with.

Clare pulled a pained expression in response to Shelley's puke in the sink. 'How's the grammar? Easy for you, I bet. You always were a boffin.'

Julie and Lotta stopped growling and stared. I smiled at them, bricking it. My cheeks were flushed and my throat felt like everything inside was being vacuum-packed. I didn't bother explaining that I wasn't pushing much beyond average in my year because I was convinced Julie Barker was going to kick my head in. And I was going to get Amy, Shelley and Lisa beaten up as well. I shrugged my shoulders, smiled and tried not to seem like I was being rude to Julie Barker's cousin in front of Julie Barker. 'I didn't make the netball team. I only play in games lessons now.'

'We should meet up in town or something,' said Clare. 'We're always down the town, aren't we?' She turned to Julie and Lotta. They looked straight at me.

'What's your name, Brainbox?' Julie challenged me to answer her question with icy-blue eyes that looked like they were starting to melt. The spliff was halfway down and tiny particles from the smoke lingered in the air. There was the faint sound of music outside the heavy town hall toilet door but complete silence inside apart from my friends' deep breathing beside me.

'Louisa. It's Julie, isn't it?'

She didn't answer and I wondered whether I should have paid Lotta some recognition as well, but Julie nodded, then said, 'Where those trousers from?'

We all looked down at the light cotton trousers I'd rolled up to three-quarter lengths. They'd got a pastel floral pattern all over them and I'd got pink lace tied in my jazz shoes. What did she want with these girly trousers? Julie Barker dressed like a bloke.

'Someone made them for me, my mum's friend's mum . . . You can't buy them.'

Julie Barker grunted, 'Shame,' kicked Lotta and turned to leave. Clare waved bye and said, for the third time, we should really meet up in town. I hoped she didn't look our number up in the phone book.

The door swung open again though, stopping them all from leaving, and two hefty men in bomber jackets and black slacks piled in and pinned Julie and Lotta against the wall. All hell broke loose as they tried to restrain Julie.

'You must think we're bloody stupid, Julie. It reeks of puff right down the corridor,' said one of the bouncers. 'Come on, girls, it's time to leave.'

While Julie kicked, spat and punched, Lotta pulled some nunchucks out from under the big long waffle-knit sweater she was wearing and started spinning them around her head with little skill or control. Both men stopped short. A teenage girl with a riotous handful of Bruce Lee wasn't something they'd bargained for. They ducked, swerved and swore until they got it together again and took Julie and Lotta on as they would grown men.

We all – Claire included – bundled into the furthest couple of cubicles from the entrance, and from out under the door watched feet lurch back and forth. Two sets of huge black boots and another two sets of slightly smaller black boots with pink and orange laces.

The air was charged with confrontation and blood pumped around my body frantically. It was the first time I'd been in the same room as people who genuinely didn't give a flying fuck about the rules, and even though it was terrifying – those girls were completely wild – it was totally gripping.

There were a few bangs as the nunchucks eventually flew off; they ricocheted against a wall and a door and then landed in the cubicle next to us. Lotta hissed at being finally apprehended. Julie was brought to the floor, straddled by one of the lumps, and I could see part of her face.

The police should have been called, but the security

guys obviously thought better of spending an hour or so with Lotta and Julie, waiting for them to turn up. Instead they kicked the girls out the front door of the town hall with a ban. Clare left too, resigned to her lot, even though the bouncers made it clear that the ban didn't extend to her.

We sat in silence on the steps in the foyer for the last twenty minutes, watching people mill around, staking out whoever it was they were hoping to get off with before home time. Eventually Amy broke the silence. 'That was mental.' She smiled at me and gave my wrist a little squeeze.

From the passenger seat of my dad's car I spotted Julie, Lotta and Clare crossing the road ahead of some traffic lights and then disappearing into the shadows. I remembered Clare's mum from school – she sometimes came in the minibus with us when we had away matches – but Julie and Lotta were, in their own way, as foreign as Madonna and the rest of them in that New York club. There's no way I could have imagined them going home for a cup of tea with their folks, and while my dad took the mickey out of my outfit for the second time that day, I became even more curious about some of the less certain worlds that existed beyond mine.

After a little over ten minutes of Dad singing along to Barbara Dickson on the car tape deck, we pulled up outside Amy's. The porch light came on and her dad Terry waved from the front door. Amy poked her head in between me and Dad and said, 'Night, Brainbox.'

She still writes 'Brainbox' on my Christmas card.

Five

Over at the small open-air stage, Bart heads straight for a girl in a flesh-coloured catsuit, dancing astride a glossy black hobby horse. Her outfit's topped off with bright red lipstick, ginormous black sunglasses and a bird's nest of blonde curls. Somehow she manages to pull it off without seeming ridiculous. She looks amazing. I, on the other hand, feel frumpy and notice that my deodorant is wearing off.

Turning up at a festival is a bit like your first day by the pool on holiday: everywhere you look people are tanned and relaxed. They know the way to the toilets and how to ask for some little fried fish in Portuguese while you fidget in your brand-new kaftan and head-scarf. Right now I'm the potato that just landed, with sand and suntan lotion up the back of my legs.

The clouds are burnt pink and gold. They are feel-good, this-has-been-a-brilliant-kind-of-day-and-the-evening's-only-just-kicking-off-clouds. The dancing hobby-horse girl is on the fringes of a crowd of a few hundred people bouncing around to Whitney Houston, belting out 'I Wanna Dance With Somebody' from a wall of oversized speakers. Back in London, the only way that half of these people would be seen dead dancing to Whitney would be by saturating the air with so much irony they'd choke, but right now, they're singing as if they're at a football match and throwing their arms in the air like they're on a package tour of Spain in the seventies.

I'm stiff, still holding my stuff, and keep losing my balance as another girl dressed as an oversized Chanel handbag, with arms, legs and head poking out from black-and-white quilted fabric, jostles against me. People have festival personas like they have holiday personas. Everyone seems to have already morphed into theirs and I've got some serious catching up to do. I feel like a prick, like everyone knows that my husband has run off. I need a drink I guess, that's all.

On cue Bart turns back round to me followed by the hobby-horse girl who offers me a murky mix of fruit juice and some sort of alcohol from a plastic water bottle. I taste it. Warm vodka and grapefruit. 'Bart managed to prise you away from Dan then? Nelson, stop it.'

She's interrupted by six foot four of gyrating crotch, complete with a flat cap and a washed-out 'Florida Keys' souvenir T-shirt with eighties graphics.

'How do you expect me to dance on this thing when you keep trying to hump me from behind, Nelson?'

Extraordinary. The show pony is in fact Helena, Bart's flatmate. It's been ages since I've seen her, and boy, has she had an overhaul. The girl I knew was a runner at a production company, lived in baggy jeans, T-shirts and chunky trainers, and was beautiful in a modest, barefaced kind of way. She'd always been up for a party but I'd never seen the pronounced shape of her bum cheeks in lycra before. No wonder her boyfriend Nelson's got the horn. Even I'm tempted to touch her bum.

Bart reads my mind, grabs the bottle from Helena and nods in the direction of a couple of upturned crates. 'She looks amazing, right? She's DJing here later too. Come on, sit down over there and have a drink. I'll vomit after that burger if I keep moving.'

We perch just a few metres to the left of two girls taking full advantage of the extra spinning-around space at the very edge. The pair, in matching navy hot-pants playsuits and French Foreign Legion hats, sing to us as we dodge their arms and I feel myself begin to relax as I smile back at them and neck Helena's warm vodka and grapefruit.

'So, what's happening? What else have you been doing, apart from taking shit from twatface?' asks Bart, lighting a cigarette.

'Making a mess of everything. I woke up in a state this morning, picked Dan up from Tom's, took a million years to get down here and got an earful from the witch about missing deadlines for the magazine's website.'

I stick to telling him about the work fuck-up rather than the work guy I nearly fucked.

I can't bear to launch into that disastrous episode straight away. I love Bart to bits and will probably blurt it all out after I've polished off the rest of the vodka. 'What about you?'

'Me and Rachel aren't speaking at the moment,' he answers. He's always rowing with her. 'She thinks she's Elvis. She wants more credit for the songwriting without doing anything. She went off on one and now she won't talk to me.'

'Fuck.' I stare at a little kid in a spacesuit and his mum sitting on the floor eating noodles out of recycled cardboard trays on the grass to the left of us.

'To cap it all off, I'm sleeping with her friend TJ.'

'Does Rachel know?'

'Not blinking likely. I won't stand a chance if that Looney Tunes sticks her nose in.'

I feel a tiny stab of platonic jealousy.

'I got off with a guy from work last night. Andrew Glass. Back at the office.' I can't help it. It just comes out.

Bart starts choking with laughter. 'You did what?'

I laugh, loosening up with the vodka. 'I almost had sex with one of the blokes who sells advertising. So bloody corny, on the meeting-room table.'

'No way.'

'Yes way . . . Please don't say a thing to anyone, not even Helena. Dan can't ever find out.'

'Do you like him?'

'It was a disaster. The guy's a complete sap. I can't believe I'm even telling you this.'

'So forget about it. Silly old tart. It doesn't matter . . .' Bart jumps up, pushes me right off the crate and, laughing his head off, starts pulling the damp, creased contents of my bag out onto the ground.

'Come on, where's your party outfit, Lou? Who's next on your list? Let's go and cruise the VIP area.'

'You wanker, Bart Coleman . . . That's the last time I tell you a fucking secret. Just piss off and get me another drink.'

Bart ducks as I chuck my roll-on deodorant at him. Straight away I wish I hadn't: not only had the bloody organic, chemical-free thing cost almost a tenner in Planet Organic, but sprawled out on the ground, I'm treated to another whiff of my armpits. It's starting to get dark, I have no idea where the thing has spun off to and Bart is on his way to the bar.

In spite of the smell, I stay lying on the ground, arms above my head, looking at the sky. The evening air is full of the sounds of people moving around, a plateau of hustle, mixed with smoke from burger vans and campfires. Beer too, I can smell a lot of beer.

Looking upward, I indulge myself in a clichéd train of thought and enjoy the idea, at least, of a communal experience with nature.

I'm brought back to my senses as Helena wedges the wheel of her hobby horse between my legs and smiles down at me. 'Fancy a spliff?'

I don't have time to answer. She's already dismounted and is skinning up on one of the crates.

'Why are you lying underneath all those clothes and carrier bags? Where's Bart?'

I shrug, hoist myself up and start to stuff everything back in my bag. 'He's gone to the bar. Did you manage to calm Nelson down?'

'Yeah, man. What a dirty old dog. Things were a bit dodgy a few months back, but now, the light's pinged right back on.' Helena smiles, lights the reefer.

'What happened?' I'm curious: last time I saw them they were slumped on the sofa halfway through their second bottle of Merlot watching *Top of the Pops 2*.

'I dunno. Well, I do. I stopped spending so much time with him, started going out with my friends a bit more, playing in a few new clubs. Chucked in my job – I'd always thought I wanted to be a director and didn't realise that I actually didn't want to any more . . .'

'And the trainers?'

'Yep, ditched them. It forced Nelson to take a look at himself and have a shake-up too. Bingo. We're not bored out of our skulls any more. Don't know how long it'll last, but hey.'

Helena passes me the joint and I inhale. She has a point. I don't actually like dope, never have done, but I'll always take a drag – I do it without thinking even though it always makes me feel slightly nauseous. Bloody Marys too. I can't stand them. I have to smile when I swallow or I'll gag, but I'll always order one with everyone else at lunchtime then gulp it down to get it over and done with.

'All right, ladies.' Bart is back, walking towards us, balancing four massive plastic cups.

'Jesus. It's boiling in this thing.' Helena pulls at her armpit.

Which reminds me. 'Bart, you didn't pick up the deodorant I threw at you, did you?'

Helena stands up straight in front of both of us and pulls at her pits again. 'God, I could do with some. Have I got sweat rings under my arms? Can you see?'

'No, you haven't, but your fanny's a bit hot by the looks of things.' Bart tilts his head back and pours half his drink down his throat. Dancing with the hobby horse has left a wet patch on Helena's crotch.

'Fuck's sake ... Oh whatever, it's dark, I suppose. Lou, do you fancy coming back to my tent with me? I need to change before I start work.'

I rub Bart's thigh, warming him up for the minor liberty I'm about to take. 'Will you watch my bags? I'm not carting them with me and then back again.'

'Go on, you old trouts ... And get a move on.'

Six

It was a complete fluke that Amy and I were in Ibiza during the summer of 1989. We weren't as switched on as we liked to think we were and the whole Ibiza thing hadn't figured on our radar. The *Sun* may have been running acid-bashing headlines for ages and smiley faces had been everywhere since the summer before but it hadn't really hit us for real; Amy and I hadn't graduated much beyond getting to know the bouncers in crappy suburban nightclubs and drinking double JDs with Coke.

For two or three years running my mum and dad took me, Amy, my older brother and his girlfriend somewhere in the Med for a couple of weeks in August. This time, as soon as the holiday ads had gone on air in January, they'd paid the deposit for a fortnight's half board at the biggest hotel in Es Cana, a small, family-friendly beach town in Ibiza.

Five days into the holiday and Amy and I were resigned to the fact that my parents had made a bum choice of location. Until, wham, nine o'clock in the morning a big group of lads with a huge stereo landed on the empty beach that we skipped breakfast every day to claim a prime spot on.

All of them had long hair and some of them had it up in funny little ponytails right on the tops of their heads. They were wearing bright, cut-off jogging bottoms and lurid T-shirts. Loafing around and shuffling about in the sand to Soul II Soul.

The minute we sat down on our towels, one of the guys – the shortest and freakiest – came over and crouched down next to us. He was in a yellow T-shirt and pea-green cut-off jogging bottoms, with big smoker's teeth and bad skin.

'All right, girls? Darren.' Darren held his hand out to shake with us. He was stoned, mellow and cartoonish.

Darren may not have been much to write home about in the looks department but he was a welcome deviation from the squabbling kids and shouty parents that would soon descend and cover the sand with windbreaks, Disney towels and inflatable dinghies.

'You get out last night too?'

Our hopes for the summer of '89 had, embarrassingly, been pinned on the Skytours brochure's promise of several bars and a disco, no more than eight hundred metres from our hotel. On the early-evening transfer from the airport several days before, Amy and I had shared a set of headphones, listened to Neneh Cherry and scoured the streets for signs of life. Apart from the odd local boy on a moped, Es Cana was largely full of pink-faced Englishwomen with tan lines pushing buggies and photo menus of giant ice-cream sundaes covered in squirty cream, set against a faint bounce of piped Europop.

We spent our first two hours at the hotel in our room, washing, scrunching and spraying our hair. Taking it in turns to use the hairdryer or stand on the balcony and listen for sounds of a party.

Out on the main strip of road through town, we walked past bars with wooden cartwheels in the stonework playing Spanish guitar music and shops selling inflatable dolphins. The only place with any potential was at the very end of the main sweep, but despite the neon signs and a terrace covered with varnished bamboo chairs and tables, it was still half empty at midnight. Underwhelmed by Roxette, Milli Vanilli and Paula Abdul, we bought a packet of foreign fags and sat on the hotel balcony.

The first few days slowly peeled away and the pair of us dragged ourselves out of bed early to nab a good spot on the sandy crescent-shaped beach: if we weren't going to be out all night dancing and snogging boys, we'd bake ourselves for ten hours during the day.

Darren talked nineteen to the dozen. He had sparkly blue eyes, like saucers. He was a shopfitter. Him and his mates were all from Essex and they'd gone straight out to a club after flying in and ditching their suitcases the night before.

They'd booked a cheap late deal on Teletext. Destination on arrival. 'We'd been hoping for somewhere closer to Ibiza town, but there's no point making a song and dance about it – it's cabs, that's all. You girls ravers?'

There had been parties at the rugby club back home where everyone did acid dancing if a house track came on, but parents picked up at midnight and no one was on it. Some of the boys mouthed off about dropping pills, but it was with the same hollow bravado that bolshie adolescent virgins rely on before they've actually had sex. Still, we all did the dance, rocking back and forth from the waist and making shapes with our hands. In hindsight we might as well have been doing the Macarena.

The beach began to fill up and Darren's fit mate Ian – taller, tanned and with a brown curly bob – came over with a spliff and a bottle of poppers. Laughing gear, Darren laughed. By the time my lips were burning at the roach end we'd arranged to go out with them in two nights' time and that – that was the start of every-thing.

It was like someone had peeled off a layer of the night and airdropped us in. Amy and I only had enough money to go to Amnesia once and we were too chicken to do any pills, but just being there was head-spinning. Everything about the enormous club and the people in it was an invitation to feel things differently.

Dancing in the open air, through the early hours of the morning, was like swimming naked in the sea, and while the music wasn't new to me, the thrill of being in the midst of a jacked-up crowd with such a powerful new spin on getting its kicks left me delirious. Even more so as pilled-up Ian began stroking and massaging my shoulders.

We didn't ever get to the beach early again: when-ever the guys weren't off clubbing, we hung out with them, smoking and talking until it got light, and when they were out, Amy and I listened to the tapes they lent us and practised skinning up.

On the drive back home from Gatwick with my family we remained silent at the news on the car radio: the police had set up the national Acid House Unit in the next town to ours. For once, living in a nondescript nowhere just off the M25 had put us at the epicentre of a storm. The BBC newsreader described how police were chasing convoys of cars around, every weekend, as tens of thousands of kids hunted down open-air parties.

At the end of the first week back at school, I made an excuse about where I'd be staying and went to a party with a giant sound system, fairground rides and twenty thousand paying punters. It was in a field less than two miles from my house. The police tried to block the roads but all they could do was look on as the mayhem unfolded.

Inside the party Amy and I hopped about in little circles wearing Ali Baba trousers and long-sleeved T-shirts, dancing on our Es to Gino Latino, checking our watches every five minutes. It was spitting and my suede boots had a black rim of mud collecting halfway up. We jumped around on a yellow smiley logo'd bouncy castle to kick-start our drugs but knew it didn't take over an hour to come up on a pill. So, with everyone else gurning and bumping into us on the damp vinyl, we sacked the party, sat in Amy's turquoise Talbot Sunbeam and put the car radio on.

No one told you when you started dropping pills that you would spend almost as much time willing on the drugs that you've paid twenty quid a pop for as you would do off your face. In those days probably half the Es I swallowed were duds, including the ones we bought from the muscly bloke with two bumbags and an Aztec-trim poncho that night.

The tickets had cost twenty-five quid each, plus there was the twenty we'd wasted on compacted baking powder. We'd got about a fiver left which we'd saved to buy water with, plus nowhere to go: Amy's car was boxed in and we'd each talked ourselves out of a night in our own beds with bullshit stories to our parents.

We sat talking and smoking on the brown leather-look seats for hours and hours. Watching bodies with sweatshirts tied around waists inch past and bums resting on bonnets fidget around. Until we ran out of fags and, eventually, things to say. Until it had stopped raining and the strobe lights gradually bore less impact onto the sky. Until Amy had to pee.

Outside, the grass was soggy and the sky was blue-grey. A huge crowd-pleaser of an Italian piano house tune coursed across bumping bodies, over the tops of the trees. I was yawning but still nodding my head along to the music when Amy came back out of the Portaloo cabin with a stupid look all over her face.

'Open your mouth.' No way. 'Girl from Liverpool gave it to me, she's already had three.'

'It's half five. We'll be off it all morning.'

I swallowed the bitter-tasting semicircle and within quarter of an hour felt its beginnings.

We found ourselves in the right place at the right time on many occasions that summer. From then on Amy and I listened exclusively to Centreforce and

Sunrise on the radio and queued on Oxford Street outside Mash and the Boot Store for Mark Wigan T-shirts and Desert Boots. We dialled 0898 numbers from phone boxes and garage forecourts, crammed into cars and shared pills. It just kept on getting better.

Seven

Within thirty seconds of closing the tent flaps behind her and flicking on a couple of torches, Helena is naked apart from a tiny, flesh-coloured thong. She has small, perky twenty-three-year-old breasts and I'm finding it difficult not to stare at them.

I've known Helena since she left school and Bart came to do work experience at my office in a misguided stab at journalism. Now she's rummaging around in her rucksack with her arse up in the air.

'What are you looking for? Thought you said you were going to put some shorts on over the top of the all-in-one?' I say to her bum.

'What do you think of this?' she asks, sitting back on her heels, raising her eyebrows. She holds up a tiny Liza Minnelli *Cabaret*-style shorts suit, minus the bowler hat.

'I love it. Put it on.'

'Fancy a cheeky line?'

'I'd love one, so long as you stop sticking your arse in my face.'

One of the other things I remember about last night was ya-ya-ing with everyone outside the pub, us all piously agreeing that festivals are brilliant because no one really does coke. Why do people always try and pull that one? Everyone's at it, at least till they're really running out of money and brain cells. Then they start on the mushrooms and all the hippy shit.

Helena hands me a wrap and a tenner and rolls around on the floor into the shorts. Why is it always the things that are so tiny that are so complicated to get on?

I chop out two lines on an atlas using my laminate and in the odd silence that surrounds friends shuffling around sharing drugs we snort them. Moments later we're sharing make-up, swapping mirrors and torches.

'Do you want some false eyelashes? Here, I've got some spares.'

I look at my eyes in the yellow light that's reflecting in Helena's old-fashioned vanity mirror. 'Why not.' I'd shown up this afternoon like I was going to a barbecue at my parents'.

As our breath shortens, heartbeats quicken and the conversation speeds up, we spend the next few minutes loading up the strips of acrylic with glue like a pair of surgeons. The music outside seems to get louder, the air inside the tent even closer and I want to get moving.

'This would look great on you.'

Helena throws me a finely beaded vintage shrug with several gaping holes in it. She's Kylie-style petite whereas I have shoulders that come from a childhood spent ploughing up and down lengths of the local pool. I squeeze them together to get it on.

She pushes through the tent flaps and I poke my head through to look at her new ensemble. 'How do I look?'

The taste of the cocaine runs down the back of my throat and I tilt my head to one side. 'Take the vest off. You don't need anything under that little jacket.'

'But, there's no button.'

'Try it.'

Helena whips it off, throws the vest at me and pulls the fitted jacket back on.

'Come on. Let's go.'

Back on the hard, stony track leading away from the tents, I feel way taller than my five feet five inches. We're striding along behind the food stalls that line the edge of the main site. The smell of chemical sweet-and-sour chicken is overbearing and I hold my breath until we're out front.

My cheeks empty and we're through the looking glass. In the time it had taken to change, the number of people in the place has doubled and every single person has decided to walk around in a different direction.

Fired up with the heat coming from the mass of bodies we've become part of, we swap speed-walking with ducking and weaving in the direction of Total Relapse.

'Shit, stop.' Helena yanks my arm and pulls me off to the right. 'Look, look, over there, that's Rachel's friend, TJ.'

I've never seen TJ before but Bart's horny description was bang on. Glossy dark brown hair, olive skin, gappy teeth and an arm full of beautifully detailed tattoos of birds. Helena's already heading over but the last thing I want right now is a stranger crashing everything. 'Helena, wait. It'll take forever to get through all those people. We'll come back in a bit . . . I really want a wee. It'll be a nice surprise for Bart. Later.'

I reach out, smile, take a hold of Helena's clammy hand. I push us back on course and any pangs of guilt to the back of my mind.

When we reach our destination, the numbers of strutting, air-punching pissed people has more than doubled there too. Everything is bigger. Everyone is loaded.

I'm genuinely disappointed at what a bitch I've been

turning into, but without looking too far I see a group of professional couples 'on a mad one', some scary, statuesque townie girls with amazing bodies and two rugby boys with their girlfriends.

Fresh air, the intro of my favourite Queen song, 'Don't Stop Me Now', subconscious relief that there are now a few more people around thirty and the drugs, of course, propel me through them, doing that half-walking, half-dancing thing.

On cue Nelson reappears and grabs Helena's breasts. He must be able to sniff out his girlfriend at a hundred metres. Bart is back too. He's not quite as happy to see me but I figure he's just flustered from pushing through the crowds.

'Save me. Those two are at it again.'

'Where the fuck have you been? You've been gone an hour, Louisa . . . I've been stuck here looking after your sodding bags. I know you stink but how long does it take to put some deodorant on?'

Shit. I'd forgotten about my bags – and my pits for that matter. I stop dancing and look at Bart dolefully, blink pathetically a few times hoping my new extensions might garner me some forgiveness. I think for a second about mentioning that we'd seen TJ to get me off the hook, but I go for the easy way out. I still have Helena's wrap in my pocket. 'Come to my tent and have a line with me.'

Finding the Boutique Field is a piece of piss. We barely slip into our stride and we're there. The security guy shines his torch right in my face and then down at the photo ID on my laminate. Bart paces around behind me, nodding his head to some tinny old reggae coming from inside the fence.

The Boutique Field is a cleaner, less cramped, chichi version of the campsite I'd just been in with Helena. A more sophisticated older sister with yurts housing champagne bars and a sushi stand. If it weren't so hot there'd have been an ice sculpture for sure. Even the grass feels springier underfoot as we walk past a neat row of tepees, some beach-style chalets until we get to a sign saying 'This Way to Bedouin' by a cluster of huge Arabian-style drapey tents lit by hundreds of tea lights.

'What do you reckon? I'm number 9.'

After a wretched start to the day, I've finally lucked out. By the time we find our way in, I'm delirious. Right in the middle of the room – there's no way you could call this a tent – is a full-on double bed with plump cushions and a satin quilt. I'm not a huge fan of the whole Moroccan interiors thing but everywhere I look there are huge swathes of bright-coloured fabrics. Rugs and cushions cover the whole of the floor.

Bart spins around, picking up lanterns and teapots, opening the mini-fridge door and shutting it quickly when he sees it's empty.

'Have you seen this?' Bart has pushed his way through a curtain at the back. 'You've got your own bog, Lou. How did you pull this one?'

I fly over to inspect the chemical loo at the rear. 'That's amazing. Christ, do I owe Alexa one.'

There were pluses to working for a hard ass after all. Alexa had gone all out at the festival publicist when she'd been told it was only broadcast that were entitled to backstage motorhome accommodation this year. I'd been embarrassed at the time, when I'd heard her rip into him on the phone and hoped he wouldn't make the connection if we crossed paths, but my old boot of a boss had pulled a corker. Screw slumming it backstage, I've made it into Grand-a-Night Corporate Hospitality and it's better than being upgraded from economy to first from London to Sydney.

This is the kind of perk that makes my crappy salary tolerable. What others don't realise is that although people on glossy magazines might look loaded, many of us rely on freebies.

Bart and I crash onto the bed. The covers get dirty straight away with the dust from our shoes. He jumps up almost as quickly. 'I'm getting us both some champagne. I'll be five minutes.'

I think about hanging some of my damp clothes out to air on the hatstand by the door but carry on poking around.

On a distressed pink leather circular sofa to the left of the bed, I find a complimentary copy of the official festival chill-out compilation, a selection of organic massage oils and a *Rough Guide to the Kama Sutra*. I flick through but the line drawings are far too abstract to make out what's going on.

I carry on pacing around and discover you can hoist up the panel of fabric above the bed so you can lie down and see the stars.

By the time Bart gets back, that's exactly what I've done. I'm far mellower than I had been half an hour ago. The drugs have worn off a bit and I'm feeling more drunk than wired. Bart settles down next to me, eyes skywards too, but as we sip from plastic flutes, all I can think is that I am staring into space with the wrong man.

'I've got something to tell you,' I begin.

'What's that? You're a twat, twatface?'

'No. I saw TJ earlier when I was with Helena. I didn't tell you because I wanted to relax and for it to be just the two of us. I'm sorry.' I don't want to admit that I've started to get on a bit of a downer without Dan. 'You ought to go and do your worst, before someone else does.'

Bart turns his head on the pillow but I carry on looking upwards. I can see him blurring at the corner of my eyes. He takes hold of my hand and mocks:

'You're a selfish cow. You're never going to sleep with me, so I've got to get my goodies somewhere, haven't I?'

'Go and get your end away,' I insist. At least one of us should. 'I'll see you at Heather and Felipe's wedding tomorrow. You better not turn up smelling like you've been shagging all night, that's all.' Bart doesn't take much persuading. He necks the remnants of his drink and plants half a dozen excited, slobbery dog kisses on my forehead, and he's off.

I lie in the same spot, briefly thinking about the way Dan used to lull me off to sleep when I got angsty, before wondering what to do next.

Eight

I soon get bored on my own and make my way back-stage to the main bar where I knock back a couple of sambucas to liven myself up and search for some friendly faces. I turn away from the bar and scan left to right. Fucking typical. There, by the entrance, talking into the ear of a youngish guy in a black vest, black cotton shorts and black plimsolls, is Alexa. It only took a few seconds for me to recognise her in one of her favourite just-graduated designer's outfits and one of those caps with beer-can holders and plastic tubes to drink from. She's got down here early – tonight rather than tomorrow morning – and is paddling palms with the young freelance writer she'd been goading me about earlier. Paul bloody Vincent, mincing around like a member of Hitler Youth in his PE kit.

The inside of my mouth is covered with a liquorice

vapour and my eyeballs push a few millimetres further out of their sockets. I sneak back out past them and set off to the media centre. I want to get online and see for myself what Vincent has written for today.

A security guard waves me into the first of three adjoining tents. Brightly lit with harsh artificial strip lights, there are a couple of empty long tables with two chairs behind each. I walk straight through and into a darkened room glowing with blue from the thunder-bolt screen saver that strobes out from each of the computers running along the walls on either side.

I crane my neck round to the last tent. It's where they do all the interviews and small acoustic sets you see on telly. If it's like last year it leads out into a little garden.

I pick up a cardboard folder with a little stencilled chewing-gum man on the front in knock-off Banksy style. It's the official press kit for the festival, supplied by one of the sponsors. I trip on a piece of loose, hard mud and lurch onto a chair in front of a computer. I see my fuzzy reflection in the screen and realise that I'd forgotten I was even wearing false eyelashes.

It takes three attempts to type the magazine's URL correctly. When our home page finally pops up on the screen the main headline reads 'The Lost Weekend Starts Now!' followed by image after image of bandalikes and attention-grabbing club kids including, I notice, the Chanel handbag who bumped into me earlier. Standard stuff. Becky, the staff photographer, has rooted out the usual mix of avant-garde, sexy and sulky.

I scroll down to the bottom, ready to rip into Paul's account of the day, when there's a tap on my shoulder. I let out a little squeal and turn round to see a greying thirty-something man wearing a filthy white linen shirt, chinos and sports sandals.

He holds onto the back of my chair to steady himself but he is still swaying, and slurring too. 'Have you seen a Nokia phone?'

I look around me and shake my head.

'If anyone does, it's mine.' The guy works his way along the surface I'm sitting at and starts picking up mouse mats and putting them down again. Then he gets down on his hands and knees and crawls around under the tables. 'Sodding piece of shit.'

I watch as he climbs back up to his feet empty-handed and tutting.

'I'll look out for it.' I smile, shrug my shoulders and turn back to the computer as he wobbles off.

I flick the mouse to get rid of the thunderbolt but there's nothing at the bottom of the home page apart from photographs. I go back to the top, to check I've not missed anything there. Not a jot. Apart from the credits. Captions: Paul Vincent. Photography: Becky Harding.

I hadn't bothered looking at the captions as I'd whizzed down through the photos. He must have done a vox pop. My booze-soaked brain can't imagine what kind of insightful question Paul Vincent quizzed the faces in the photographs with. Must have been a blinder by the way that he and Alexa were sidling up to each other.

If I weren't so pissed I'd be too insecure to look and would lie in bed the next morning feeling paranoid about whichever blinding witticism he'd spun out. Instead I look straight under the first image, then the next five or six.

What the fuck? He's done a name, age and town job. Becky got those details as standard whenever she shot anyone.

I'd been balled out over a caption story. If that's what she'd wanted in the first place then Alexa could have put a fucking work experience kid on it. Not me, and not Paul poxy Vincent.

I drum my fingers on the desk, push onto my toes so I tip back in the chair and stare blankly at a laminated poster attached to the tent fabric behind the monitor. I check my phone. Still no word from Dan. I know what I'm about to do is inane, but begin to do it anyway.

I tap in the remote access code for the website, which allows staff to update text when they're working out of the office, and delete the names underneath the first shot of a group of Led Zep wannabes. I replace them with 'Cuntface, Cuntface, Cuntface and Cuntface, all 24, Ipswich'. I read it through for typos and carry on. This time, for a girl in a Perspex bikini, I go with 'Titwanker, 21, New Cross' and for the Chanel handbag '26, Dalston'. So it goes on until I exhaust the lowest dregs of my vocabulary and everyone has a new name. I press save, foolishly happy that it'll cause a minor eruption tomorrow.

I light a Marlboro Menthol, now semi-paralysed by what I've just done.

A noise coming from the back room stops me from replaying run-ins I've had with Alexa in the past. The lights in there have gone out. I'm in half a mind to leg it out to the security guard at the front but dash in, switch the lights on and stand frozen to the spot. A redhead I recognise vaguely from the arts desk at the *Daily Telegraph* is getting stuck in to the bloke who'd lost his phone, the pair of them snogging like a couple of fourteen-year-olds while their parents are out.

They're a damp mess of crumpled neutrals. Both of them look at me with a childish mischief that is wrong for two people in their thirties.

'Whoa . . .' I stare hard at them, looking for some response but get nothing. 'You didn't find your phone then?'

Still reeling from hitting the save button, finding it difficult to speak, it's the only thing I can think to say.

The guy raises his eyebrows, shakes his head. As I leg it out and over to the bar again, I realise I know the guy's face too. He's a late-night weather presenter. He must be down here in the hope of a mudslide.

Nine

Looking back, I wonder how I became so utterly jaded.

'I want to write ... about music, fashion, people, anything new, you know?' When I was in my teens that's what I used to tell anyone who asked, and a load more who didn't. It was the truth.

Working on a fashion magazine seemed like the only way I'd ever get out of Kent for good and find my own Get Into the Groove world of feathered hair and thick eyeliner.

I liked the thought of bashing away at a keyboard, working to a deadline somewhere important. The practicalities of being an actual working journalist, as I discovered, weren't quite so glamorous.

For an afternoon a week during the sixth form I compiled the schools pages of the local paper. The novelty of knocking on people's doors, being told to bugger off and writing about German twin town exchanges quickly wore off.

After writing barely a word, academic or otherwise, a couple of years later as a student I landed a stint of work experience at *Bite* magazine. It was one of a handful of publications to emerge hot on the heels of others like *Dazed & Confused*. They all covered similar territory: new designers, cutting-edge photographers and avant-garde bands who sold a handful of records.

I'd just finished my second year at university and for two weeks I took a break from lifeguarding shifts back home, caught the commuter train into Charing Cross and pitched up at the *Bite* office in Soho.

I'd got in there by a stroke of luck. In the midst of planning my dissertation in the spring I'd written a letter to the editor on the off chance. A month later I got one back asking if I wanted to come in.

After reading every back issue I could lay my hands on, I turned up on my first day in my best Bella Freud dog-print T-shirt and jeans with carefully blow-dried hair and a notebook full of ideas. I spent the first morning opening the post.

No one really seemed to be doing much and everyone was smoking. The editor Pippa scribbled away in her diary and told the girl that answered the phones not to put any calls through to her. Alana, the fashion editor, sat with her feet up on her desk flicking through an enormous leather-bound portfolio, while simultaneously arranging crisps in an open sandwich and puffing away on a cigarette.

The office wasn't what I'd expected, more like a series of small rooms on the second floor of a narrow Soho building. It was on a corner and from one side of the editorial office you could see a row of grubby net curtains. From time to time one of the hookers would poke her head out and smoke a fag in the fresh air.

The other girl doing work experience with me was called Aurelie. She spoke three languages fluently and often did. 'I'm at St Martin's,' she told me. 'I'm doing fine art.'

I didn't know anything about art school; I was studying English, at a very straight and academic university, and became instantly seduced by Aurelie's straight-talking brand of sophistication.

She was at *Bite* for the whole summer and filled me in on how it all worked. The magazine was run on a shoestring and almost everyone who contributed did so for nothing, to get noticed. 'If paying to get cutting-edge work out in *Bite* means you get picked up by Italian *Vogue* or you land the next PlayStation campaign, it's a small price, isn't it?'

'I'd love to run my own magazine eventually,' Aurelie announced while we were on the sandwich run, on my second day. 'There's a smell that you get when you flick through a freshly printed magazine. The ink is really pungent but it only stays like it for the first few hours. There's nothing else quite like it.'

My ambitions weren't so entrepreneurial. I knew I'd never be cut out for a proper newsroom, but I was still in love with the idea of writing and set my sights on eventually turning in front-page features and interviews for the broadsheet supplements of the Sunday papers.

I spent at least half of the first week at *Bite* with my nose in the *A to Z*, as I dropped off and collected clothes, portfolios, artwork, salad boxes, even Pippa's house keys to her boyfriend who'd got locked out. It didn't matter.

Trawling around Soho, in and out of tens of buzzy buildings that would be a dream to work in for their energy alone, after two years in the Midlands at college, was immense. I carried on adding to the list of editorial ideas in my notebook but it didn't matter that I hadn't written a word, for real, all week. I felt part of something, even though I quickly realised not much in the way of work really got done at *Bite*.

All kinds of people – fashion kids, twenty-something tabloid aristos, convicted poets – popped in and out during the day to hang out. The art director Henrik never showed before two and then just sat staring into his sketchbook.

At one point Alana explained to me: 'Doing nothing is part of the creative process.'

I quickly learnt that going out and getting tanked up for free was also regarded as a valid part of the creative process. Every day when I opened and sorted the post there was a wad of invites to a never-ending merry-go-round of launches, private views and parties.

I often think if I told people what went on at *Bite*, they'd never believe me. Over the weeks I realised they were all crazy and were probably incapable of working anywhere else, but I loved it. A cub reporter post at a local paper would be hard work and the people would be sensible. *Bite* was a lifestyle and infinitely much more fun.

I was gutted when my last day came round. On Monday morning someone else would be in my chair.

I watched everyone buzzing around, sparking off the Friday afternoon build-up to the weekend, but I'd also been warned that we'd be in the office until God knows when tonight. After a lot of talking shop and partying, a month's worth of actual work had been crammed into the last three days.

My eyes were burning from poring over pages. I'd been checking for typos and missing credits on and off for hours. At half one Pippa told me and Aurelie we might as well chip off and sent us on our way with a couple more invites for parties the following week and a tenner for a cab. Everyone was knackered but smiled, thanked us for getting stuck in. I felt deflated and watched out of the cab window as we made our way through west London to Aurelie's.

I realised we were in her road when she sat up on the edge of the cab seat and began craning her neck. 'Fuck. Shit. Fuck, fuck, fuck . . .'

There was an ambulance parked up with the lights on. A medic was talking into a radio. Aurelie jumped out the cab the minute it stopped, gave the driver the tenner and ran along the pavement up her path. I followed as fast as I could. Aurelie smoked like a chimney and from the sound of her chest didn't ever run far. She jabbed inside her bag for her keys and said, 'The fucking plumber. I locked him in. I told him I wasn't going to let him leave till he fixed the fucking water.'

'You did what?' She was totally barmy. I couldn't stop laughing.

'Don't. He's probably fallen out the bloody window trying to leave and broken his neck or something.'

She ran to the side of the house and back again. My hysterics subsided as the colour drained from her face.

Inside, halfway up the communal stairwell, two green-overalled ambulance men were lifting a wheelchair down towards us. I became immediately convinced the plumber had collapsed with a stroke.

'Is he OK?' Aurelie was beside herself, not so big

and clever after her bolshie trick had backfired on her. 'My flatmate was meant to be back by five.'

The first medic looked confused. 'Him? Mrs de Souza has had a fall, suspected broken hip, eh, love?'

'What about the plumber?'

'Plumber? No, this is definitely Mrs de Souza. Isn't that right, love? Would you mind stepping aside for us now, ladies?'

The plumber had left hours before, down the drain-pipe, by the looks of things, said Joel, Aurelie's flat-mate. The woman coming down the stairs was the old lady from the top flat.

With the hot water back on, my fortnight at *Bite* had come to a dramatic end, befitting my new friend.

A week later I dropped by the office to collect a copy of the new issue. My name was on the masthead along with Aurelie's and a couple of other interns from previous weeks. I got my first whiff of that just-printed smell Aurelie had told me about. I was hooked too.

Ten

Back at the VIP, the surprises continue. Dan is standing hand on his left hip, right foot out in front. He's got a cigarette in the other hand and tilts his head back when he takes a drag. The jeans he was wearing earlier are cut off to the knee.

I watch him for a moment from the entrance as he banters with another bloke in hard-to-find, expensive Japanese streetwear. The guy pulls a punchline and holds his head in his hands, looks back up and holds his hands out, feigning disbelief. Dan creases up. The laughter lines that cover his face spring back again. He holds his stomach, screeches like a chimp and hops around. It's a fine line between alpha and boorish but these two have got it down.

I spin a pearl bead around and around at the front of Helena's shrug with my finger, sway a bit uneasily on my feet. I should be psyched up for some argy-bargy but Dan's done it again. He's making me feel nervous, coy, and I start backtracking, giving him the benefit of the doubt, when I should absolutely, I know, give him what for and then ignore him for the rest of the weekend. Sometimes I think I left my balls back in Kent when I left home, went to uni and ditched the Estuary twang.

I make my way inside. I stop right next to Dan who 'All right, darling?'s me and pecks me on the cheek. His face is looking rubbery close up. I smile at the other guy who gives me a small nod then carries on talking. I wait for Dan to introduce me but he puts a hand on my shoulder instead and they continue. It's warm and gentle and when he lifts the meshy fabric and rubs between my shoulder blades I can feel the rough skin he says comes from being an apprenticeship on a building site. He's smoothing out my prickles and nervous energy but I'm not a flaming Labrador.

'Dan,' I snap. 'Sorry about this . . .' I apologise sarcastically to the guy in front for interrupting him ignoring me. 'Where've you been?' This is pointless. I can feel myself smiling at him. Dan's in raffish mode; the chemicals in his brain are throwing high fives with the ones he's been throwing down his gullet and up his nose. I don't want to row with him when he's like this, not this weekend, and he bloody well knows it.

'Chris, this is Louisa, my missus. She writes for *Neon*.'

Chris makes proper eye contact with me this time, holds out his hand and adjusts his stance to make the conversation three-way. 'Nice one.'

I would moan to Bart about it at some point but accept his acknowledgement of me as the wife, rather than the unfortunate bint his new mate might otherwise have been shagging. Of course, the revelation that I am, in this particular landscape, someone oils his manners too. Not that I'm above a bit of that, it's plain that he's no ordinary punter either, so I give him a collusive smile.

'So, what happened?' I ask.

It would be counterproductive to say anything else and I want an in. Dan's on top form, hanging out with someone whose future doesn't look like it might bottom out with a crack pipe, and I want to share the ride, come on board, be at the same party as my husband for once. We're in with a chance of spending the early hours lying in bed with racing, happy hearts rather than scratching around for more drugs with a bunch of strangers. The last time we both managed to get home together without being totally wrecked had been a reminder of why we got together in the first place.

Dan smirks back at me. Eyes puffy but, what green I can see, still bright. 'I couldn't find you . . . Louisa,

I'm sorry. You know what it's like. This place is straight off the dial. I got carried away.'

'OK, OK. What's the fucking point? There isn't one. Who wants a drink?'

The other guy doesn't hear me. He's too busy shaking hands and back-slapping with another alpha, a bit younger, in dirty skinny white jeans and a loose-necked white T-shirt. The rude shit can get his own drink. Dan strokes the side of my face and whispers in my ear. 'Nice one, Lou ... That guy, it's Chris Sellers.'

Chris Sellers made his name as a hot young producer during the late nineties, sold his label to one of the majors and has spent the last few years counting the pennies, despite moaning to anyone who'll listen that he has been creatively short-changed.

Dan is more than pleased with himself for notching this one up. Chris isn't even thirty yet, he's three years younger than Dan and he's exactly the kind of guy Dan is desperate to be like. Probably the kind of guy I'm desperate for Dan to be like too, if I'm totally honest, not a part-time Top Dog who grafts at a tatty restaurant for eighteen grand a year.

Dan leans in and kisses me on the mouth, his hand moving over my shoulders again, down to my waist, into my shorts and onto my bum. I flick my tongue slowly around his. My eyes are closed but I see abstract bodies jolting and twisting around to an old punk track. I hear the hum of grinning faces.

Dan finally leans back, rubs both lips together and keeps his palm on my bum cheek.

'I'll have a beer. Meet you back here in five.'

No prizes for guessing where he's off to. 'Dan, don't get too wasted.'

He looks down at his shoes and back up at me. 'Do I look fucked?'

I take his hand out of my shorts. 'Please.' I don't know if I'll win or lose this one tonight, but I've got to remain optimistic, and if I keep him with me now at least I can see what he's up to.

By the time I've got back from the bar, Chris has edged over into a bigger group of identikit white-jeaned rakes, which I recognise as the latest unsigned band at the centre of yet another overhyped bidding war.

I find Dan in the less desirable company of a high-lighted bag of bones from the past and he's irked and tetchy after being shelved by Chris for the boys from the band. I can't remember Charlotte's surname, prob-ably never knew it, but I would never forget the first time I met her. It was my first proper encounter with one of those scratchy, insincere people who seemingly exist to make everyone feel uncomfortable with one another at the tail end of a long night out.

It was the morning after Princess Diana died and

we were all still up round someone's house doing liquid acid and watching the telly. It was a dark day and she made it even more horrible by shaping little factions and stirring up snappy arguments around how the remainder of the coke got shared out. In between dropping hints to all of the girls that she'd had casual sex with each of their boyfriends in the past. Nice.

Dan didn't deny shagging Charlotte when I quizzed him a few days later; he tutted, said it was when he was at college and he didn't know any better. He warned me to keep clear of her and from then on I gave Charlotte the cold shoulder whenever I saw her out and referred to her at home as Shagalot. She kicked around for a while, never really with anyone except whichever DJ she was sleeping with at the time (house music was big then) until, I think, she fucked off abroad somewhere.

Now, with long blonde hair framing a face with sunken cheeks, sporting a long white ribbed vest as a dress and a crazy look in her eye, I catch Charlotte feeding Dan bumps of coke off the back of her hand. The old dog realises she's barking up the wrong tree when she sees me turn up with our drinks, kisses Dan on the cheek, excuses herself and moves on.

I don't dwell on it, though, because now my hair is dripping with water. Dan grabs his nose as a stream of water hits that too. Both of us carry on wiping drips away, looking at each other, up, down and all around.

Again, right on the back of my head, I feel a cold blast.

'Where's it coming from? Someone's chucking water.'

'No they're not. Look, your cavalry's arrived, Lou.' His tone's caustic.

He points over to the right. 'Behind that group of girls.'

I jump up and catch a glimpse of Bart and Helena, armed with a couple of water pistols. Helena had finished her set and is on a mission to take Bart's mind off TJ: Rachel had spotted them together, kicked off and broke up the party. So Bart and Helena are cracking off iced-water hits in the VIP instead.

Dan increasingly tolerates my friends with the same disdain I have for most of his. As the pair of them stand giggling alongside of me, Dan leans over, snatches Bart's toy gun and starts planting shots at random people. The joke quickly wears thin and an unremarkable but well-spoken young guy holding a walkie-talkie and wearing a T-shirt with the Banksy-style chewing-gum man I'd seen on the press kit earlier edges his way in front of us. His hands are in his pockets and he nods towards the guns, suggesting an end to the squirting. 'All right, guys. That's it now. Couple of girls over there are a bit upset with you.'

Helena, Bart and I bite our lips and look past him.

'What, mate?' Dan's voice immediately gains some

edge and my stomach falls through the floor. I look sideward at him and can virtually hear what is going through his head: No clueless fuck's telling me what to do.

'Dan, leave it. Let's go outside for a little while.' I pull at his hand and he throws it up in the air, eyes boring into the mousy, apple-cheeked bloke in front of us. Goading him to keep pushing his luck.

'Look, guys, it's my job to make sure everyone has a good time tonight. That's all.' He fails to cut through Dan's irritation with the pally, let's-all-be-decent-blokes line and resorts to pulling rank. 'Can I see your pass please, mate? Everyone back here has to have a pass.'

Without the one he should have collected from my friend Ramona earlier, whatever line Dan trotted out to the girl with the clipboard and the list on the way in isn't going to wash now.

'Don't know where I've put it, mate. I had it, and now I haven't.' I look at the aggravated shapes my husband's mouth is making. The testiness to the way the words are falling out of it.

'Look, let's not cause a scene. This area's for VIP guests only, that's all,' says the guy. 'What's your name? I can check it on the list and everyone can go back to having a good time.'

He radios over for the girl with the clipboard. After a bellyful of Dan's attitude he's clearly enjoying calling his bluff and cutting him down to size. The thirty seconds we spend waiting for her to show up are excruciating. People nearby are sneaking glances over. My heart is in my mouth.

'So, who are you then?'

What a tosser. The next few seconds, while the guy looks up and down the long list of names, become unbearable. Before he finishes telling us what we all already know, Dan erupts.

'Fuck you. Piss back off to the rest of your graduate mates in Clapham.' Dan squirts water from the fluorescent-pink piece of plastic into the middle of the crowd. The guy leans in and tries to take the gun out of Dan's hand, but my husband has been given the excuse he was looking for to kick off and fires up.

Dan shoves the guy staggering into a group of girls nearby. One big, hefty, long shove. We should get back to the tent now, I want to say, turn in. I pull at Dan's arm again and he shakes me off. Harder this time.

The guy pulls himself up onto his feet, apologises to the girls behind him and holds his hands up, in another effort to reason with Dan. It only makes my husband angrier. For a split second it looks like the bloke is about to throw a punch and, this time, that's it. Dan explodes, lurching in and headbutting him. The guy drops straight to the floor, clutching his head, knees into his chest. It's disgusting.

Friends have whispered reluctantly that lately you never know whether you're going to get Nice Dan or Nasty Dan when you go out, but in less than a minute he's gone way beyond nasty, far beyond a bit of coked-up growling.

Dan once told me about a fight he had outside his local pub when he was seventeen. He gave someone a nosebleed after he found out they'd been seeing his girlfriend behind his back, but that was it. Nothing like this. The grotesque display taking place several feet away from me is off the scale. All the poor sod on the floor can do is hope it's over quickly.

Like a city-centre thug caught on CCTV, the speed and silence with which Dan lays into him on the floor is blood-curdling. Something I've never seen anyone, let alone the man I share a bed with, do within close range. A quick series of ugly jolts from his knee down to his Converse, smacking into the guy's fingers, his face, his hair.

The pound-shop water pistol is cast aside on the grass. It takes a while for me to register that the hysterical woman screaming 'stop' over and over again is actually me. Everyone directly around us is looking down, stunned at the split-second shift from midsummer optimism to this, while elsewhere people carry on laughing and drinking, oblivious.

I barge through the crowd until I find the only man here with bigger balls than my husband.

'Quickly, you've got to come. Dan's in a fight. I swear he's gonna kill him.'

Chris Sellers pushes through, stony-faced, with the five boys from the band close behind, probably hoping that someone from the *NME* sees them. Dan has already run out of steam, and is beginning to regain normal levels of consciousness.

As Chris and the others wade in and haul Dan away, the sweat coming off his body is like that of a race-horse as its ribs expand and contract after the finish post. I run over and look into Dan's eyes. He's finding it difficult to focus.

'You need to disappear fast.' Chris shunts me out of the way and pushes Dan into action. 'Get out of here, before the Old Bill turn up.'

Eleven

I watch, suspended in a gloopy haze of utter disbelief, as a pair of medics place an oxygen mask over the bloody nose and mouth of the guy on the floor. I feel the viscous sensation of physical detachment that morphine brings, but still with all the pain of the here and now.

I can only just hear what Helena is saying; my ears feel like airbags have blown up into each canal. It's as if she's on the other side of the glass in an eighties double-glazing advert. She's telling me his name's David Lester, that he's the marketing assistant for a new chewing gum, Minty.

The music plays on and as I look away into the middle distance where pints are still being poured, I'm struggling to get to grips with how quickly everything kamikazeed. My brain isn't allowing it to register.

David Lester's girlfriend's mates are trying to hug her as she kneels down by his side, tears streaming down a face contorted with crying. One of them is standing up, pointing out into the darkness, sternly gesturing to a security guard as another spits into his walkie-talkie.

Behind them I see Alexa, surreal in her novelty hat, staring down at the blood-spattered, pulverised young man on the floor, then up, straight over at me. Her sad, disappointed eyes say she saw it all.

Bart lights me a cigarette and wedges it between my fingers. 'The prat's really gone and done it this time.'

I feel a firm hand on my shoulder. It's Chris. He turns to Bart. 'Mate, why don't you get her out of here?'

'We need to find Dan. Make sure he's OK.' I flinch as I think of how absent my husband's expression had been before he'd sprinted off.

Bart ignores me, leads me outside. Heading towards the backstage exit, we don't say a word. I try Dan's phone but it's switched off.

Bart stops to buy a couple of bottles of water from a middle-aged crusty, sat in the darkness by the side of the path with a battered plastic cool box. Passing one to me, he finally breaks the silence. 'Just think of all the great outfits you'll get to wear on the prison visits.'

I erupt, crying, weeping, hold my stomach, try to lift one heavy leg after the other until there's nothing I can do but jolt around on the spot. My nose is running and I can taste snot as it goes into my mouth. Mixed with saliva, I dribble as I try unsuccessfully to speak, gasping for breath.

Bart wraps both arms tightly around me, forces me to stop rocking, breathes in and out deeply, encouraging me to do the same. 'I'm only joking, you div. Now, come on, breathe . . . Have some water.'

'Do you think the police will have found him by now?'

'Stop winding yourself up. Fights always look worse than they are. Let's just get back to the tent and calm down. There's nothing else you can do. Honestly.'

I know Bart's right and with wobbly legs carry on walking with him until we arrive. How has it come to this? I should be dragging Dan back here for a hot, sweaty shag.

I sit on the bed, hugging my knees, smoking cigarette after cigarette, running my hands through my greasy hair. Everything's still slightly blunted by the booze but it's becoming sharper. Bart lies next to me, looking up into the night sky. I close my eyes and wince.

Twelve

I watch Dan line his ingredients up carefully on the wooden kitchen work surface and smile – spring onion, coriander, lemon grass, carrots and ginger. The last time he made Thai food was on my birthday.

There is a saucepan full of boiling water on the gas hob. He adds some jasmine rice to it and then steps over towards the bin to discard the empty plastic bag. The kitchen floor is covered with broken glass and I hear it grind against the wooden floorboards as Dan moves around. The big kitchen window that accounts for most of the end wall is wide open – it's warm and dusky – and a Grace Jones track that I don't recognise is playing in the background.

From my seat at our small wonky-legged kitchen table I look at the sprigs of hair on each of his long toes. Bare-chested, his old camouflage trousers are rolled up so they're sitting just above his ankles and shards of glass lie on the outer edges of his flip-flops. I look back down and carry on leafing through the newspaper in front of me.

There's a battered old champagne bucket from the restaurant on the work surface too, filled with a selection of 'knives' – jagged shards of broken glass of various sizes, brown, green and clear. Dan picks a small one and begins chopping. The knife he's using breaks midway through the lemon grass and he tosses the pieces on the floor behind him. A piece lands by my foot and I kick it away without looking up from the paper.

Dan replaces the broken knife with a much bigger one. The sound of it scraping against the metal of the ice bucket puts my teeth on edge.

I ask Dan if he wouldn't mind keeping the noise down a bit while he's getting me my dinner ready. He grinds more glass into the floorboards on purpose, stepping over towards me to give me a little kiss, and says, 'You just keep reading, eh, it'll be done soon,' and then grinds back again to his chopping board.

The music changes and Dan throws himself on the floor, break-dancing.

His small muscular torso quickly becomes covered in cuts and scratches, but I gently encourage him with a short burst of lazy whooping and faux cheers before returning to the paper.

Our neighbour from the basement flat is poking a huge stick – a broken branch from one of the trees in his garden – into our window and shouting at us to turn the music down. I don't want a row, I'm not one for confrontation, but Dan doesn't care and pushes the volume up a couple of notches. He's had enough of him complaining every time we switch the stereo on.

Back on his feet, Dan is picking splinters out of his chest and dusting himself down. He throws the rice, spring onion, coriander, lemon grass, carrots and ginger into a wok. There's a big whoosh when he adds some soy and then an even bigger one with a dash of fish sauce. The whole of the kitchen is full of smoke but the whooshing noise quickly subsides and the smoke starts to evaporate. Dan adds a sprinkle of pepper and a dessert spoon of sugar. He flicks a clove of garlic out the window into the garden below then asks me to get some forks out on to the table.

I pour two long glasses of San Miguel from a big litre bottle, tip my chair back and reach into the cutlery drawer. Dan's fingers are bleeding and tiny drops speckle the rice he spoons into the bowls we normally eat cereal from. He garnishes the dish with some fresh coriander and then sprinkles broken glass over the top.

There's been blood before, back when we first met, but never glass in the food he's served up to me. I scoop up a forkful and start eating anyway. I watch

Dan do the same. The familiar taste of the classic garlic–coriander–chilli mix is quickly overpowered by the sound of crunching in my head.

I'm woken by the sharp pain that comes from biting down hard on my own tongue.

Thirteen

I'm awake but keep my eyes closed for a bit. As the connecting threads of my brain fuse back together and the flashbacks cut in, I'm all over the place.

I had a breakdown in my late twenties. After the mother-of-all-party binges, I left Dan at home and curled up on my parents' sofa. He'd tried to straighten me out but I was in a real mess and he couldn't take any more time off work. Each night Mum and Dad took it in turns to sit up in the armchair next to me, ready to stroke my head, steady my breathing and hold my shaking arms and legs. I bounced back quick enough after a few months and got the job at *Neon*, but it's cast a shadow. Ever since, I've struggled to control the bouts of anxiety-charged convulsions and manic episodes that can kick off the morning after a big night out.

Sometimes I have a theory that I work with for a

while. That the spasms in my arms and legs, the habit I've got of pulling out clumps of my hair, all the crazy, humiliating impulses, are all down to one ingredient from the night before which I then go on to exclude. For instance, that as long as I don't drink pub wine, I'll be fine the next day. Or by steering clear of coke if I'm doing pills, I'll spare Dan the dawn histrionics. Occasionally it works. Occasionally after compensating for missing out on the coke, I take so many pills I end up in casualty. Sometimes I think the only answer is to knock it all on the head but that never lasts long either.

The last time I woke up in the same bed as Bart after a night out, I was so beside myself I launched into a headstand against his bedroom wall. This morning I'm rigid, bar a shake in my right index finger. Bart is complaining about the light streaming in from the open panel above the bed. Neither of us moves to shut it. Instead he gets up and curls onto the leather sofa hugging a bottle of water.

'How you feeling?' My voice is small.

'Blah. What about you?'

'Awful.' Dan hadn't just made a bit of a show of himself last night. In one fell swoop he obliterated any claim he might have had to the lovable rogue tag: he had upgraded to violent headcase. 'Where do you think Dan went to?'

He rolls his eyes, takes a huge gulp of water. 'It'll blow over. The guy wasn't that hurt. Dan was just venting. I need some coffee. Want one?'

I nod. 'Black, no sugar.'

Bart pushes the huge fabric door wide open and more unwelcome sunlight blasts through. My finger carries on bobbing up and down as I conjure up snapshots of Dan asleep at the bottom of a grassy bank next to an A-road. It's still sinking in, what he's capable of, and I feel a needling sense of guilt and shame by association.

Bart's soon back with the coffee. It's already perked him up. 'Get this down you and take a shower. You can't lie in your pit all morning dragging up last night's dregs.'

He's right. What Dan did was despicable but I have to find a way to get through today without losing it. I wish I could just get the hell out of here but I need time to straighten out my head before I get over to the media centre to do my interview. My index finger and middle finger start scissoring as I remember editing the *Neon* website. If I screw this interview up, Alexa'll fire me for sure.

It's not only work that's brought me here this weekend either. My friends Heather and Felipe are getting married later today. For real, on-site, at the festival's temporary Chapel of Enduring Love, by a legitimate minister surrounded by their friends and families. They met down here two years ago when Heather, a photographer, was covering the weekend with me for *Neon*. People might think it's all a bit tacky, the kind of thing that tabloid pop stars do when they're off their heads, but getting married properly at the Lost Weekend makes absolute sense to my friends. Heather would never forgive me if I didn't show up.

'You know what – I'm going to the Star Children's Field. Do you fancy it?'

'I'm Jewish, remember?' yawns Bart. 'We don't do Christmas or yoga. Call me when you're done. I need to go back to my tent.'

It's only ten thirty but it's already scorching and the place is jammed with weary sunburnt faces that made it to bed in the early hours but are unable to sleep another minute in their canvas greenhouses.

The entrance to the Star Children's Field is a small opening in a tall hedge, with just enough room for two or three people to pass through at a time. I'm greeted by a man in white robes handing out photocopied guides to the series of gardens and little outhouses that play home to a mishmash of treatments, therapies and hocus-pocus. He's wearing a sticker that says 'My Name is Wolf Pixie Sky' and has the dead-eyed look of a hired festival freak shipped in because the real freaks can't afford to come here any more. I imagine him picking up the garb from the employment agency early this morning together with a crib list and his box of leaflets.

'How are you healing today?' he asks.

'I don't know . . .' Where do I start? For a brief moment I think about telling him that my husband's beaten the living daylights out of someone, I've sabotaged my work's website and I'm in the yoga field trying to ignore how everything has gone so horribly wrong. Instead I take a leaflet and walk straight through.

I go past a mix of reiki, shiatsu, reflexology and cupping tents, until I get to one that says Psychic Sisters. I'm sorely tempted to get my Tarot read but I carry on walking, in no shape to handle any more knocks. I'm here to give myself a break, not fill my head with even more shit to worry about.

The garden's relative stillness is comforting. I need more of it. Not the group couples' counselling circle, that's for sure, but one-to-one meditation looks promising. Ten pounds for some peace of mind.

The woman on the rattan mats, Barbara, is reassuringly businesslike and centred. More chippy than hippy. I like her straight away. Looking good for early forties, at a guess, in black Nike yoga pants and a black vest; her only concession to her holistic bent is a toe ring. She looks straight at me through steel-rimmed spectacles.

Her voice reminds me of the estate agent who sold me my flat; feminine but no bullshit, first-generation white collar. 'Have you meditated before?'

I say not really, a bit at the end of a yoga class I used to go to. She asks me what it is that I'm looking to get out of this session and I start waffling about how hectic my life is, that I'm here covering the festival but I'm frazzled and I need to get some focus. I know full well I ought to be brave, to be honest, for her to help me, but decide to lie and stick with the generally stressed-out line.

'Right then,' says Barbara, dimming the light. 'Let's see what we can do.'

After some breathing and relaxation exercises, she asks me to close my eyes and to visualise the place where I'd most like to be. It could be a beach, the countryside, she prompts.

'Just let go and allow it to come to you.' Barbara's voice is lower, slower, verging on monotone.

Through the blackness my mind brightens and I climb a lone narrow tree trunk over a hundred feet high. It has no branches, apart from the cluster that sprouts like a kid's Afro at the very top. There are no other trees around and among the branches stands a simple birch-wood tree house.

The whole thing is Heath Robinson lite crossed with anime. Inside the tree house I look out through the windows. I can see for hundreds of miles across pale pink, lemon and light green villages, towns and cities, with steeples and monuments springing out into the sky, until the earth curves right at the edge of my frame of vision. I get off on being up so high, being able to see so far, but am soon distracted by a snake on the window ledge.

I hear Barbara asking me to lie on the floor wherever it is that I am, to be aware that the tips of my toes are relaxed, that my ankles are relaxed, then my shins, my knees, thighs, groin, pelvis and so on, until we reach the crown of my head. Then she asks me to take a deep breath in, letting it run all the way down my spine and then all the way out again, up my spine, over my head and out between my eyebrows. Continue to do this for a while, she says. My mind is suspended in the new place that it's found. Through the blackness behind my forehead, energy expands outwards. I find stillness.

Eventually the time comes to ease up onto my feet, climb back out into the branches and shin back down to the ground.

'I really felt you needed that,' says Barbara as I open my eyes. My head feels lighter, my whole body feels lighter, less frantic. The darkness that set in after Dan's explosion of violence last night is still framing everything but I've got some space to manoeuvre, do what

I need to do. I'm ready to start picking up the pieces with Alexa.

'Oh my God, Louisa, what are you doing here?'

I'm supercharged with pragmatism and oxygen from all the deep breathing, but it begins to subside the moment I recognise the slender six-foot Asian woman coming towards me. I'm instantly pricked with unease. It's my friend Amita, holding a piece of paper with a drawing on it. She gets closer and I can see it's a self-portrait.

Amita is looking more delicate than normal, still a carefully put-together, confident high-end Essex Asian with a smattering of bling, but as she approaches she's remarkably slower and more considered than even a few months back. I notice her Tiffany charm bracelet is replaced with traditional Indian silver bangles.

We hug in a non-committal way and it feels odd. We've been friends for years, since we were stuck next to each other at a birthday dinner and both Dan and her equally nonchalant, skint ex-boyfriend made it obvious they didn't care much for our mutual friends. Eventually they disappeared into the bar next door while Amita and I forged an alliance. From then on we regularly made a dysfunctional little foursome out and about until just before Christmas when Amita and Jonathan split up.

'I've been meditating,' I say, keen to promote a sense of introspection that I know Am has already been smart enough to crack on with.

'Oh.' Amita seems surprised and changes the subject to the piece of paper she's holding. 'Laurie and me are working on some stuff. This morning's been kind of to do with that.' Laurie is Amita's therapist. She's always been bolshie but since the split with Jon, who she always assumed she'd end up marrying and having babies with, she's lost her temper on a few too many occasions in the office, potentially sabotaging her reputation as one of the most talented and forthright PR pros in London.

Provoking bouncers outside clubs to remove you from the pavement outside their premises when your own clock is running is one thing, but suggesting to clients that they're badly dressed starfuckers is another.

'Louisa, have you seen anyone else?' Amita's voice wavers. 'I'm not so sure it's such a good idea to be breezing around the place.'

'What are you talking about?' Like I don't know.

'Dan's in a lot of trouble . . . The police were all over the VIP last night, taking statements.'

I scratch my head and repeat Bart's flimsy mantra. 'It'll blow over.'

'I don't want to scare you but Dave Lester is still in hospital. They're serious injuries . . .' She nods her head apologetically, then looks to the floor.

Hospital. I can feel the blood start to fizz around my veins. My eyes fill up. 'You know him?'

'His boss used to be a client. People are talking about it, Louisa. They know who you are too – everyone knows bloody *Neon*, don't they? I honestly didn't expect you to be around.'

'I can't just go home, Am, I'm working – and it's Heather's wedding too. Besides, I haven't done anything wrong.'

'I'm just telling you what people are saying. As your mate.' I'm already resigned to the fact that I will be the subject of endless backchat among the cliquey media crowd gathered here this weekend. She gives me another hug, this time more solid. 'Fucking blokes, eh?'

'Thanks for being straight with me.' I try to gather some perspective: surely I can handle a busload of muck-rakers from London among the hundred thousand people who've come here? 'I'll leave you to it . . . You look really well, Am.'

I hold my head up high, prepared to take whatever comes my way from the snipers. I've got to focus on the hour ahead of me, on pulling it out of the bag to make amends with Alexa. Then I can show my face at the wedding and split.

I stride resolutely past the line of beach huts in the Boutique Field. All I need to do is to brush my teeth and grab my Dictaphone. Coming towards me, however, are two thickset police officers. I've made my way back without being hissed and booed at but I didn't reckon on these two. I stupidly try to convince myself Dan's been in an accident.

'Mrs Taylor?'

'No. Well, yes. I'm Louisa Parker. My husband's Taylor. Is he OK?'

'Where is he?'

'That's what I'd like to know.' I raise my eyebrows.

One of them coughs, unamused. 'We need to ask you a few questions. About last night.'

I look at my watch, back up and across at both of them. I become convinced I'm going to break down. Out of desperation I try it on. 'Will it take long? I'm due at work in less than ten minutes. Can we meet back here after that?'

'Madam, a serious assault has taken place and we have strong reason to believe your husband has something to do with it. A young man's lying in hospital on a ventilator and we need to find the person who put him there. So we need you to answer some questions. Now.'

This can't be happening. I look at my watch again, over at my tent and back at the policemen helplessly, desperate for some slack.

'Mrs Taylor. We have a number of witnesses who claim your husband is responsible for this attack. The only place you're going is over to the Police Unit. Unless you want us to arrest you too.'

Fourteen

Heather's brother Marcus is doing a reading. I tuck in behind the last row of wedding guests in the rickety plywood Chapel of Enduring Love and sit on a table with my knees up under my chin, hands keeping my dress neatly into the backs of my thighs underneath.

I'm late to the chapel because the police had kept me for over two hours asking questions, taking statements, regularly leaving me sitting waiting to watch the minutes tick by. The phone in my pocket is on silent, vibrating on and off with calls and messages from the publicist of the band I should be interviewing. Bang goes patching things up with Alexa.

For once, there was nothing I could do to pick up the pieces for Dan. For the first time I began to understand the real extent of the mess, of this, of everything. I felt utter disbelief at being grilled by the police and

I felt disbelief at how low we'd sunk. GBH. People go to prison for GBH. A guy is in hospital, right now, because Dan lost it. What would we tell our parents? What must David Lester's parents be thinking about the person who did this to their son? How did this happen to us?

Not everyone wants babies and Cath Kidston tea towels, but how did our brand of chaotic hedonism become so scuzzy and nasty?

The truth is that Dan and I have turned into the couple most normal people probably wouldn't want at their party any more. The ones who used to be a right laugh, but lost the plot with the gear. The social hand grenades: me with the crazy old panic attacks and him with his temper. I want to hit rewind and make it all better. Make it go away.

David Lester is in no fit state to press charges yet but the police will be doing so irrespectively once they've nailed the guilty party.

I trod a fine line between digging Dan a hole and being vague enough with my answers to feed a basic instinct to protect him, claiming I became hysterical as soon as it kicked off and couldn't remember much. I explained how rammed the bar had been, that we were all a bit pissed and Lester had made a pig's ear of chastising Dan for something insignificant. I couldn't recall much beyond that.

The police back in London had already paid a visit to our flat a few hours ago but there'd been no sign of Dan. In the meantime they grilled me for clues as to his whereabouts. Their guess was as good as mine.

Right now, in the chapel, all I can do is keep a lid on it. People can ask each other how I had the nerve to sit through a wedding when my husband had stuck someone in hospital and was on the run from the police once Heather and Felipe are away on their honeymoon. There's no way I'm letting Dan hijack their big day.

I've known Heather for years now. She started out as a photographer around the same time as I began making inroads as a writer and we've been put on more jobs together than I can remember. When I think of her, I think of a wide grin, a pretty turned-up nose and buoyant, genuine positivity.

Once the police had finished with me, all I wanted to do was jump back in the car, race up the motorway and hide away in the flat, but I can guarantee Heather would spot I was missing. She'd been texting me all week, full of excitement and last-minute details. So here I am, a ball of nerves at the tail end of a hangover, fidgeting, at the back of the festival's pop-up church.

Tom and Zoë have made it down here, impressively after the state they'd been in yesterday, with what's best described as a loose tribute to Faye Dunaway and

Warren Beatty in *Bonnie and Clyde*. Looser on Tom's part who's visibly suffering with withdrawal shakes in a T-shirt that's already stuck to his back, topped off with a cravat and trilby, compared to Zoë in a cream beret, soft short-sleeved blouse and cream gloves finished off with a neckerchief, pearls and a fan.

It's impossible to miss Amita a few rows back in a vivid cerise sari, haughty with her big nose pointing straight ahead like she's stuck on the front of a ship. The only crack in her façade is the hand she's got placed in the rear pocket of the lanky black guy next to her, who must be her plus one. The rest of the row, mainly pretty girls from the PR agency where both Amita and Felipe work, look unfairly bland and high street in comparison.

Right in front of me there's a more pared-down and considered bunch of guys, a couple with girlfriends, spread over two rows. I take a guess that they're from the design consultancy where Heather gets a lot of her commissions from.

Marcus introduces a little girl in a Liberty-print dress who starts singing 'Daisy, Daisy, Give Me Your Answer Do'. Heather and Felipe's parents look on from the front row of plastic chairs. Felipe's mother in a hat and dress she'll never wear again from the John Lewis formal-wear department next to her husband in a similarly robust charcoal suit. Both in contrast to

Heather's mum Linda, on her own, in a red Diane von Furstenburg wrap dress.

Heather and Felipe are holding hands, backs to everyone, facing the bearded IT consultant and weekend humanist minister in shorts and sandals they've brought down from London.

Heather's long fine mousy hair's been pumped up with heated rollers and the off-white lace straps of the fifties sundress she's wearing sit on lightly tanned shoulders.

It was always going to be a difficult one to call but, rubbernecking around the chapel into a cluster of floaty dresses and hair decorated with summer flowers, partnered with hit-and-miss flirtations with men's formal detail, almost everyone has risen to the occasion in their own way.

The couple turn to each other and start their vows. Heather first, holding a creased piece of A4, gulping for air, squishing down the tears so she can get the words out. I twirl my wedding ring around my finger remembering my own wedding day.

Dan and I got married on our own in a room off the lobby of a small, intimate hotel in Ubud, Bali. We'd decided we weren't going to invite family and friends. It was about him and me; neither of us was big on an ostentatious display. It would be romantic in a way that was fitting to us.

We'd loved telling all our mates the story of how we decided to get married. England had beaten Germany and we were in the pub off our faces on pills. Dan got carried away, said how about it and I said yes. Nothing soppy, nothing poignant or considered, rather a fly-by-the-seat-of-your-pants approach to making the biggest commitment of your life.

We'd explain, over and over, that the next day when we woke up, it instantly hit us that we'd already phoned both sets of parents with the good news from the pub and the wheels were in motion. That was it. We were getting married.

In reality, behind the bravado, the episode had given us an unexpected fast track to a place we both instinctively wanted to be but hadn't realised, let alone talked about it. Getting married hadn't been on the cards but the minute it became a possibility we jumped at it and were both surprised at how comfortable people like us could be with the prospect.

From the off it was a bold dramatic statement which would hopefully also, in time, be equally as simple. Neither of us felt any great need for a religious aspect and, in retrospect, it was surprisingly easy to avoid speaking about why, exactly, we were going through with it, or what it would mean to us afterwards, but we threw ourselves head first into it. Swept along in the excitement in the run-up to the wedding it genuinely felt like the right thing for us to do. I'd also hoped deep down that being married would anchor us somehow, then maybe push things on a little.

Dan had slipped out of our hotel room during the night before our wedding and I woke to find him heavy-lidded, sat at the bureau a few feet away from the bed. He was burning some kind of local amphetamine – which he later admitted he'd bought from the concierge in the early hours – along foil and inhaling it through a straw.

I locked myself in the bathroom and downed white-wine leftovers from the night before, as I threatened through the door to slice chunks of my hair off with Dan's razor.

Miraculously, we made it out of the funk and changed into the suit and dress each of our parents had bought for us and got downstairs to the hotel lobby. There was no service. Just a quick preamble by the hotel manager before we signed on the dotted line and the manager's assistant presented us with the rings I'd bought with my Barclaycard on a pink-and-gold Balinese silk cushion. In the photos taken by a local photographer our shiny faces are smiling. We haven't looked at them since.

We checked out straight away afterwards and hopped in a car to the airport and onto a tiny little plane to Lombok. We crossed the jungle to the other side of the island in a minibus and then, finally, over to another small island on a fishing boat for a full-moon party.

You hear about it happening. Sex nosedived for us the minute we were married. Rather than Dan throwing me on the bed and giving me a good seeing-to, which is basically all I'd known up to that point, we both sat down on the mattress of the bed in our beach bungalow like a pair of wooden book ends and set about sealing the deal. Very slowly, we both took our own clothes off, and silently, with an intensity of detachment that I've since learnt to be only possible between two people having sex, got it over and done with. Maybe it was something about the prescribed set of circumstances and behaviour that meant, on that day, we went through the motions rather than made love.

A much more welcome surprise came with a knock on the flimsy bungalow door. A band of familiar faces filled its frame; I started bawling and Dan yelped with delight. Tom, Zoë, Am, Jon, Aurelie and her boyfriend Bob threw confetti, jumping up and down on the spot, cheering, waving bottles of champagne they'd packed for the trip.

They'd thought better of crashing the ceremony, but after checking with both sets of parents that no family noses would be put out of joint, they had travelled halfway round the world to spend the rest of our wedding day with us. I was totally floored.

Early evening with my wedding dress back on, we drank champagne and popped pills on the beach, warming up for the full-moon party. I could literally feel myself glowing, filled to the brim with conviction about life, love and friendship, and when big, fat warm raindrops slowly began to fall from the sky I lay outstretched on the sand with my eyes closed, content to drink in the buzz around me.

As we stepped out onto the dirt track that led down to a cluster of beach bars for a couple more rounds of pre-party drinks, the large tropical raindrops felt like they had swollen to the size of tennis balls. By the time the track had widened, we joined tens of travellers and locals wading knee-deep through a small road that was now a stream.

The freak weather was causing flash floods and in the middle of hundreds of wringing wet bodies news spread that the party was rained off. By that time we were already twatted and Dan, T-shirt and shorts stuck to his body, disappeared somewhere to try and get some more of the stuff he'd been smoking earlier at the hotel in Ubud.

He went AWOL on our wedding day. Even then. When I began to get upset and anxious everyone set off in different directions to track him down. Which is how I came to spend my wedding night with Steve from Leeds who started talking to me after I got freaked out by the shadows of some sleeping cows.

Steve quickly got bored with helping me look for my husband and suggested we headed back to his beach hut until it got light again. I had no option. I couldn't remember the name of our bungalow or which direction to head in. Steve had been taking amphetamines – pills, powder, even some over-the-counter semi-legal fizzy drink – and the hours passed with him reading me extracts from the diary of his year travelling.

I got my own back later that morning by presenting him with one of my self-loathing seizures. All I could think about was my mum's tears at Heathrow as she'd waved us off.

The sun came up as Steve helped me find the way back to my bungalow. Over the course of the morning Tom, Zoë, Am, Jon, Aurelie and Bob gradually assembled back at the same spot of beach we'd started on the day before, each with a story to tell. We looked out at the day from under a tree, watching the sea. Eventually I spotted Dan bowling up the beach with a bottle of vodka. Typically, he glazed over any detail of where he'd snuck off to with a line about being caught up in some vague nonsense or other. Time had melted away.

Before I had a chance to give him any kind of grilling, though, he took me aside and made me close my eyes and hold out my hand. I felt my husband gently kiss my forehead, my cheeks and then my shoulder before pulling me towards him and fastening something lightly on my wrist. 'I got this for you.'

I opened my eyes and saw a small bracelet of shiny black beads around my wrist, with a heart-shaped bead in the middle. It had the same kind of metal screw clasp that held together the necklaces I brought home from holidays as a kid.

'Look closer, there's tiny bronze glittery bits in the beads, they're made out of a kind of volcanic rock or something . . . I love you, babes.'

As the rain that would continue to fall for the next three days descended again, the nine of us (Steve from Leeds included) necked more pills and threw ourselves around on the sand. The bloody bracelet Dan had given me eventually snapped while we were midway through a handstand competition on the beach, but I managed to find most of the beads plus the wire they were threaded together by. I got them all the way home to London and they're still in a little pot by the side of our bed.

Looking on at Heather and Felipe, surrounded by family and friends, both crying as they exchange rings, I slip mine off and hide it away in my purse.

As everyone files out of the chapel I hold back until it's safe to make my escape unnoticed and puke on the grass around the back.

Fifteen

The guests edge down the steep hill away from the chapel, led by a small fully costumed Napoleonic marching band which bears no relevance to either family tree but that announces the new Mr and Mrs Valdez passing through the crowds with a bang.

The procession bowls along, at the very back of the audience singing along with the band on the main stage, until we cross into the Meadows, an expansive grassy retreat away from the mayhem of the main site with a small lake and clusters of trees. The drummers grind to a halt to the right of a canvas canopy sheltering cups of Pimm's and Heather's mother stands on an upturned crate, with a half-empty plastic cup already in her hand inviting everyone to get stuck in. Still queasy with the acidy taste of sick in my mouth, I hang back under the shade of a tree, battling the urge to slip off and hide back in my tent. It's one thing to want to do the right thing and show face for Heather and Felipe but it feels wrong to be laughing and joking at a wedding when that guy, David Lester, is laid out on a hospital bed only able to breathe with the assistance of a machine. All because of my husband and his raging temper.

I did, however, decide to come here so I need to get a grip and play along. I look over at Amita as I fiddle with my bottom lip. She's been through a really messy, protracted break-up but she's still raising a glass to her friends and gazing into the eyes of a bloke she doesn't really give a shit about.

'What you up to over here on your own?'

I hadn't noticed Zoë heading over to me. She shoves her Pimm's in my hand and flaps the fan she's been carrying around with her so that we both get some air. The round edge of the fan echoes the curviness of her small frame. 'Quickly, before Heather's mum canes it all.'

She raises her eyebrows and I smile weakly and shake my head. I can't stomach it.

'I heard about what happened.' Most of my weekends are spent with Zoë, listening to her chatter non-stop through the night while Tom and Dan call people they haven't spoken to in months then cab it across town and back again. She talks so much that once, in a club,

I collapsed and Zoë didn't even flinch, she just carried on rabbiting as I slid down the wall I'd been backed up against. Bless her though, she was still there at my hospital bedside when I came round, talking about God knows what.

But today all she says is 'I heard about what happened' and waits for me to say something back. I don't often get to enjoy her more considered side. It's a shame. It would be nice to see more of her in the week.

I shake my head, rub my eyes. 'I feel terrible.'

Zoë thinks before she speaks. 'Drink that and stick a brave face on it. It's that or you'll start hyperventilating. I'd go for the brave face.'

She's right. Its smell alone makes me gag but the Pimm's rinses off the film of vomit still stuck to my tongue and, stoically, we head over arm in arm to Bart, Helena, Nelson and Tom.

Up close Tom looks even sweatier than he did in the chapel but Tom wouldn't be Tom without a bit of sheen and a twitch. He's still fiddling with the deep red cravat Zoë's made him wear. His almost black crew cut is as dark and short as Zoë's hair is long and blonde, and he's as damp, hairy and bear-like as she's fragrant and petite.

Bored out of his mind by almost a decade as a recruitment consultant at various temp agencies around town, Tom's always got something on the go to smooth the edge off. A couple of pints at lunchtime, a can of Stella on the bus on the way home; he even swigs chilled cider if he wakes thirsty in the middle of the night during the week.

It's odd how everything bad agrees with someone who is such a good guy. His face is often sweaty yet rarely twisted. Tom has an innate sense of loyalty and kindness, and people – especially strangers when we're out – quickly warm to him, but it's all at odds with a man who also has a ravenous appetite for drink and drugs. He's Dan's best mate and while we share some sympathy for what a liability he can be, we also – or did until recently – share an appreciation of his more appealing side. Only a week or so ago they were lumping furniture from a van into Tom's little sister's new flat and riffing off each other's funny bones with stupid jokes and quips, so relentlessly that they eventually collapsed into a heap and were trapped by the velour sofa his sister had bought at a car boot fair. In the end Zoë and I fell off the wall we were watching them from too.

Straight away Zoë has Tom fetching another round of drinks and he lumbers off to get them in, tugging away at his cravat in the heat, relieved he can have a legitimate scout around on the way for anything he might be missing out on. Tom's like Dan, he likes to slip off, but the difference is he's a happy drunk and you know he'll be back in half an hour.

Helena, Nelson and Bart have already raided the fancy dress trunks that Heather's costume designer friend Sylvie has put together. They've gone for eighteenth-century France, in a vague tribute to the theme set by the band. Helena is balancing a sky-high white wig on her head and Nelson a wiry white ponytail tied with a tatty piece of black velvet ribbon. Both have pencilled exaggerated beauty spots on their cheekbones and are fanning themselves. Bart, love him, looks like an Italian teenager on a school trip to London with his court jester's hat on.

Tom's soon back, hands full. 'I wouldn't count on it being a free bar later. Who's got a bag?'

He pulls out a bottle wedged down between his bum and the waistband of his jeans. Zoë swipes it and stands it on the grass in between her feet.

The sound of drums crashes back for an instant and we're all ordered to take a seat on the grass for lunch, which comes and goes in a blur of popping corks and cold roast chicken. As the order of ceremony rolls on the drinks slip down more easily and I've stopped biting my nails. Glancing around, we could be sat in the banqueting suite of a golf club or country house on any Saturday afternoon in the summer. Only the rumble of sound systems and hubbub of the crowds bouncing around the fields on the other side of the hedge give the game away.

By the time the speeches start, Tom is resting back on his elbows, feet out in front of him, beaking around at the guys plugging in leads to the speakers around an LED dance floor on the grass behind us. He starts fiddling around in his pockets and Zoë coughs, badly disguising the rustling that's taking place.

The bag of pills passes from clenched fist to clenched fist. Bart, Helena, Nelson, Zoë and Tom make a mixture of pantomime coughs, sneezes, yawns and stretches.

I duck out. Even I'm not stupid enough to do that to myself given the circumstances. I love pills, just not today. I think about Dan in his navy-blue short-sleeved shirt, unbuttoned all the way down. I'm dancing with him in the sunshine. It's the middle of the afternoon and we're at a club in Ibiza. He's resting his forearms on my sunburnt shoulders, my hands are at either side of his waist and he pulls my head into his chest. A blurry memory dominated by our matching sunglasses and red noses.

After Heather's mum and Felipe, Nicholas the best man stands up. My ears start to glaze over and I watch the bubbles float to the top of my drink, distracted now and then by Bart as he fidgets around next to me or by Tom checking his phone every few minutes on the other side.

Eventually I straighten my back, squint and make a concerted effort to focus on what is being said until along with everyone else I give up and turn to find out what the fast-approaching dust cloud of shrieking and yelling is all about.

Coming towards the picnic at breakneck speed is a herd of twenty or thirty naked men and women, beating their chests, throwing their arms in the air, shrieking war cries like Native Americans in an old Western. The stampede is heading straight towards us and absolutely everyone (besides Tom who is sending a text) is paralysed by its force.

Soon, the mass of naked flesh heading our way becomes more defined and we're grinning like witless wonders at the abundance of flaccid cocks and bouncing boobs, all painted dayglo. The hippies are having a *Braveheart* moment and it looks like we, with our Habitat blankets, are the invaders.

Just as they become dangerously close and a couple of the children start crying, the herd swerves collectively without the slightest break in pace and bypasses our encampment. All heads turn to the right and cheers start to fill the air as the cohort of fluoro bottoms surges forward onto its true target.

As they throw themselves into the lake, the entire wedding party jumps to its feet and breaks into wild applause. Over the top of it all, the best man Nicholas rounds off: 'Now you lot know the lengths I have to go to genuinely get your attention. That lot'll do anything for a tenner a piece.'

Guns N' Roses start screeching out of the speakers behind us.

'Would you all please join me and raise your glasses one more time for Heather and Felipe . . .'

The wedding party erupts and, despite the slow start, I'm swept up in it too. Cups are filled right to the brim and girls rush the dance floor. Bart's got something else up his sleeve though. He and Zoë grab my hands, pull me to my feet and hot-foot it down to the lake, Veuve dribbling from both corners of my mouth as I try and swig the fizz from the bottle while I run.

Barefoot we squeeze into a flimsy rainbow-coloured kayak Bart spotted abandoned in the reeds. Still with the jester's hat on he's at the front, Zoë's squished in the middle and I'm at the back. There aren't any oars so we've each got a stick that we plunge downwards into the water and shunt ourselves along with.

Bart and Zoë give it some welly, punting along in time to the music bumping out from the wedding disco. I can't keep up, ditch my stick, fuzzily drunk, happy to listen to them babble on. Zoning out, my hand trails through the water at the side of the boat. Just as I'm debating whether Heather's mother bought her dress from Selfridges or Harvey Nichols (she looks more Selfridges, more provincial nouveau than footballer's mother-in-law), I whip off my shades and raise the alarm.

Floating right next to the kayak is an enormous, dark brown, bobbly poo, decorated with foam around the edges. I spent every summer as a student working as a lifeguard at the local pool back home and I've seen a lot of poo, children's mainly, and this one, with its substantial girth, definitely began its life inside someone old enough to know better.

Zoë makes a pig's ear of pushing it in the other direction with her stick and winds up splashing us all with tiny drops of water. She and Bart try to turn the kayak round but with brains like custard they reverse, leaving me closest to our attacker, holding my breath, covering the neck of the champagne bottle with my palm.

Anyone would think we were colonials, in a black-and-white movie, fleeing cannibals down the Congo. Bart and Zoë lever themselves forcefully out onto the bank with their sticks and chuck them in the water, leaving me to lurch at the grass and miss the side, planting both feet, legs knee-deep, into the sludge at the bottom.

I hoist myself out, legs speckled with algae and the bottom half of my dress dripping wet, while the other two run like the clappers, laughing their heads off, up the gentle slope to the flashing underlit dance floor. I belt it up there too, dizzy from holding my breath for too long in the boat.

Almost everyone is squeezed onto the red, yellow, green and blue squares, joining Heather and Felipe at the end of their first dance. I slide on, leaving a snail trail of dampness, showering feet and ankles with the drips from my dress as I push through to dance with Bart and Zoë.

'Do you think I could get electrocuted on this floor?'

Sarah Jane, who works with Felipe, flinches and edges just out of reach as I try to steady myself on her shoulder. I keep clanging into people but if I stay in one place for too long I'll slip over in the little puddles collecting around my bare feet. Soon enough, though, someone else goes arse over tit behind me. Thank fuck it wasn't Felipe's granny.

I watch as a girl around the same age as me in an expensive-looking shift dress with an ugly graphic print is helped to her feet by one of the design guys I'd spotted in the chapel.

She's talking loudly at her boyfriend so I can hear. 'I don't know what the hell she's playing at. Look at the state of her.'

I'm just about to wade in, suggest she'd have a better

time if she chilled out a bit, when another one of the guys she's with steps in front of me.

'I've got a better idea.'

The guy looks at me, amused but savvy enough to give me an exit strategy, and directs me back onto the grass and away from the dance floor.

'Maybe you should try the fancy dress?'

I look down at my dress and my dirty feet as we head over to the trunks of clothes. It's way too early to get away with looking like this. What on earth am I doing? 'Is your friend OK?'

I look at how clean, crisp and well laundered his old-skater-boy-done-good outfit is in comparison. How his lace-up orange Vans make his feet look small. His side parting. Laid-back but neat.

'You don't remember me, do you?'

Shit. Surely I hadn't slept with him years ago? I stop and look hard into his face. It's a tiny bit on the chubby side for me. Not fat but none of the bone structure that I usually go for and there's no way his shirt is hiding a six-pack like my husband's. His eyes aren't bad though; he has really long curly eyelashes.

I scrunch my face up, cover my mouth with my hand and shake my head. Even if I'd had a drunken shag with him, there's no chance I could tell when, where or what his name was.

'It's Louisa, isn't it? You came and interviewed my boss, Mark Ellis.'

Mark Ellis is the head of the sexiest design agency in London and headed up a star-studded collaboration between London Fashion Week and the Design Museum earlier in the year. I smile, pretend I remember who this guy is. 'Of course.'

I'm sure he's sussed I don't know and we're doing that silly dance people do while one fishes around for clues to the other's name.

'Our useless receptionist had fucked off somewhere. I made you a coffee.'

It starts to ring a few bells but I can't honestly say that I can place him, although there is an echo of something familiar about him.

'That was it,' I lie. 'Your boss pulls it off every time, doesn't he? Fashion week was amazing.'

He doesn't answer me. He's too busy rifling through the fancy dress. I lean in and rummage too.

'I'm really sorry, I don't remember your name.'

'Matt.' His voice is muffled and I can only just hear until he stands up properly. 'It's Matt . . . What do you reckon to this?'

He holds up a twenties vintage tennis outfit but it's far too narrow at the top.

'I'll never get it on.'

Matt sits down on the edge of one of the trunks,

smoking, until I come across a black short-sleeve dress covered with hundreds of giant strips of shiny black foil draping down from it. It's like a bird from outer space suit but once it's on it should be fine.

In fact, the dress is perfect. I can't wait to get rid of the old one.

Sixteen

It's about nine as the sun starts to disappear. Matt caught me just in time. The pit stop over at the fancy dress has worked wonders and I love the way the disco lights bounce on the shiny black foil strips hanging from my new frock. Time has slowed back down again to a more reasonable pace, my focus is restored and I thank Matt for stepping in. I recognise the oversincerity of someone who has had too much to drink in my own voice and raise my eyebrows. He laughs. 'No damage done – just stick with the water for a little while at least, will you?'

I wave a plastic water bottle at him and, keen to move things on, change the subject. 'Did you see anyone good play last night?' I say, quickly name-dropping a couple of bands of the moment I had managed to miss, neglecting to mention what I'd been up to instead.

'I hate festivals. It's not my bag.' Matt realises he's cut me dead. 'Sorry, that was harsh, wasn't it?'

He tells me about the time he saw one of the bands I'd mentioned years before they were signed at a tiny gig with five other people, and how he prefers small intimate venues to the brouhaha that surrounds big-name acts at huge events.

I nod and make suitably impressed noises. Matt is a bit of a music nerd but seems genuinely enthusiastic rather than a show-off. He starts on about another band he'd checked out earlier this year in New York. 'You'd love them too, I'm sure. I think they should be releasing an EP over here at the end of the summer. Pitchfork gave them a nine point one rating.'

I've no idea what he's talking about. Ever since Dan had more or less banned me from touching his vinyl and started talking over me whenever I joined in with him and Tom in guessing where a sample came from, I'd passed almost all my music-related post and phone calls on to Jason, *Neon*'s music editor. I only agreed to interview a couple of bands this weekend because Jason can't physically stretch to everything Alexa wants covered.

Somewhere along the way in our house music had turned into something men talked about together while their blonde wives and girlfriends listened. Which is bizarre. I grew up with a dad who raced home every

Saturday to play me whatever he'd snapped up in Our Price. In fact even after I left home, up until he got sick, Dad'd call me and play me bits of stuff he'd bought down the phone.

So I find myself in strange territory. Matt's interested in my opinion in music, even though I'm the stupid cow who peaked too soon at the wedding reception. It's disconcerting and the thought crosses my mind that Matt's trying to hit on me, but he isn't. He's blown his nose three times really loudly into a black-and-white Stussy handkerchief already.

I've become an expert at spotting that light when it's switched on, and Matt's, with all that nose blowing, is off. It's not one of my best qualities, but I have developed a habit of stringing men on if they give me half the chance. Bart loves reeling off the little band of dick-led editors, DJs, club owners and actors I've egged on over the years, pumping up my ego. Nothing ever happens (snogging the office square on Thursday night was a genuine first). Mainly bouts of late-night texts, drinks to discuss work we never really plan to do together and sneaky lines in cubicles at private members' clubs. My husband can be a twat yet I'm nothing but faithful.

In any case, Matt is simply making conversation, after doing the decent thing and stopping two girls from having a row at a wedding. With everything that's happened to me in the last day or so, he's also unwittingly slipped me a temporary pass back into the normal, law-abiding, still-standing upright world. All with a bit of chit-chat about bands.

'I think we ran something about that lot a few issues ago actually,' I lie, attempting to look vaguely knowledgeable and cool in front of the man who saw me thigh-high in frogspawn a little under an hour ago.

I feel a bit queasy and, from nowhere, finish up my sentence by burping the taste of garlicky home-made hummus into my mouth. Matt chokes into his pint, but tries to cover it up. I'm mortified.

'I'm so sorry. I pigged out on the hummus at lunch – I hadn't eaten since yesterday.'

Matt gives me a friendly little punch and steers the conversation gentlemanly away from me. 'Do you know what? I hadn't even heard of hummus until I went to college. My mum's family is from Ireland and we grew up in Essex. She only ever did meat pie, shepherd's pie, bangers and mash and chicken casserole. Then spaghetti bolognese too when we were a bit older.'

I look up at him and smile, worried that my breath stinks too. I know what he means about hummus.

Matt's unsettled though. His phone keeps buzzing and it's needling him. He stiffens up, drags deep on the red Marlboro he lit the moment he stubbed out the last and starts fiddling with a toggle on the bag he has with him. I try and make out what the white letters on the little red tab on the pocket of his short-sleeved black shirt spell out. It's not a label I recognise.

He stuffs the phone down at the bottom of the rucksack and pulls out some plain black Havaianas. 'Here, put these on.'

I have no idea where my own shoes are. The flip-flops are just a size or so too big for me. 'Whose are these?'

Looking down at Matt's orange trainers again I remember that his feet looked a bit little earlier. 'The flip-flops are mine.' He clocks me checking out his feet and laughs with resignation at what God gave him. 'And these are original Vans from the eighties. I brought a few spare bits with me for the day. I'm not camping here.'

He's got a room at a B & B a few miles away. No wonder he's so well turned out, although I get the feeling he always is.

I ask him about the Vans – I know people who collect rare Nike's but never Vans – and he lets on he's a vintage freak. He's an old skater and collects the shoes from back in the day. Matt starts explaining the difference between the ones on his feet and the ones you get in the shops. His ones just look a bit pointier at the front to me, but apparently there's a lot more to it.

He collects rare denim too, Levi's mainly. He talks about model numbers, stitching, pockets and buttons. Little shops in New York, LA and San Francisco. 'I've never had it all valued but, as a collection, it's got to be worth thousands. I wear some of it, the 502s and the 505s.'

It's good to hear that his interest extends beyond hoarding wildly expensive old jeans for the sake of it. His mates think he's nuts to wear a pair of jeans worth two grand until they literally fall to pieces but he can't see the point of collecting for collecting's sake. He loves the design, all the stories behind each pair of jeans or jacket, and it strikes me that it's been a very long time since I've talked socially with anyone (except Bart, maybe) about anything but work or going out. I don't dare tell him that I was introduced to the curator of Levi's own collection at the brand's press office once but was so hung-over I feigned mild interest for five minutes before making my excuses and heading off to Pret for an egg sandwich.

Matt steps back and looks me up and down. 'I've got an original girls' Foremost jacket from the fifties, the same style as Marilyn Monroe made famous. It'd probably fit you, you know.'

I look down at myself a bit awkwardly and shrug. I don't bother reminding him that I'd probably wreck it. He was making an observation, not an offer.

He tells me the most valuable thing he has is a little kid's jacket – one sold a few months back for over ten grand and he's been trying to work out if his is in better nick.

'I'm sure it is,' I say, trying to give the impression of some authority. Like I'd know. Still, even the flip-flops he's lent me are in good condition compared to the battered wafer-thin pair I've kicked about in for the past few summers. I start to feel more firmly grounded on the thick black rubber. More focused on steering things forward from my clean-up job.

'That's it. This is where the conversation about the denim obsession ends. Before you start thinking I'm an even bigger nerd than I am,' says Matt, abruptly. 'Who are you here with?'

'That lot you saw me skidding around with on the dance floor,' I half lie. He asked who I'm here with, not who I came with. 'The one in the hat's my mate, Bart.'

Before we get any deeper Amita strolls over. I pray to God she doesn't say anything about Dan. 'What have we got here then?'

Am heads up the Channel Six PR account over at her agency, Ellis Associates do all the design work and they must cross paths from time to time. Ours is a small world.

Minus her plus one, she's swaying around a tiny bit

and rests her long slender arm around my shoulder to anchor herself. Her bangles get caught in my dress.

I laugh nervously as Amita leans into me and fingers the foil strips just by my tits. She gets a bit sapphic when she's had a few. 'Nice dress, Lou.'

Thankfully, Matt is distracted by the non-stop vibrating handset still eeking away at him from the bottom of his bag and he starts digging around for it again. Once he's pulled it out, he concedes to whoever can't wait to speak to him and shuffles off out of earshot.

It gives me enough time to drill into Amita that, under no circumstances, do I want her or anyone else to mention Dan and last night. I lay it on thick and she backs off from my garlic breath. It's not for my benefit, it's for Heather and Felipe. I've made it this far and I don't want to start contaminating the atmosphere now.

She nods over in Matt's direction. He's pacing around, head down, looking slightly deflated. 'It's probably his girlfriend. I hear she's a real cow, which is odd, because he's lovely. Unless you're a client, and then Matt gives even me a run for my money.'

According to Amita, Mark Ellis has flat-out banned Matt from going to meetings with at least two clients. He's one of the agency's big-shot art directors and has got a reputation for nights out that end with flaming sambucas and boiling over when marketing people make dumb comments about his work. Especially if he's been to the pub at lunchtime, or rowing with his girlfriend. 'Anyway, I don't know all the details about her. I should probably keep my mouth shut . . .'

Am is always gossiping. I shake my head, urging her to carry on quickly before Matt's back.

'She never turns up to things when it's his friends, but she's always sticking her claws into him when she's on a downer. You know, one of those girls who look great but are mental. This one's all sixties parents and happy pills.'

For someone who didn't know all the details, Am's done pretty well.

We stand staring at Matt – shaking our heads at his girlfriend's poor show of mad, needy female behaviour, as if neither of us had ever been prone to equally unappealing displays – until he paces back over and resolutely buries the handset into his bag.

'Anyone want another drink?' He looks as if he needs one.

A familiar, gravelly voice comes from behind. 'You probably ought to, Louisa. I've just been catching up with your husband after last night's floor show.'

I feel the colour drain from my face and my eyes dart about, searching for a glimpse of Dan. My heart is pounding so hard it feels like it will rocket through my sternum.

All I see, though, as I turn round is scrawny Charlotte Shagalot, twirling her split ends around a bony finger, as she launches a saccharine smile at me. Bart, Tom and Zoë are standing behind her. What the hell is she doing here?

'Where is he?'

Charlotte's breasts, tiny sacks of limp skin, flap visibly from behind the loose fabric at the top of her halter-neck jersey dress. I get the feeling she loves the fact she knows more about my husband's whereabouts at this point in time than I do.

Tom steps forward, big sweat rings under his armpits, and turns to Charlotte. He knows her from way back too.

'I don't know why you had to tell her, Charlotte.'

'Tell me what?' I spit. Tom looks away and shakes his head.

'He's up at the farm. There's a party going on there all weekend. I'm surprised at how many of the boys I ran into.' Charlotte carries on choking me with her poisonous tittle-tattle. 'Dan's there. With Steve and Alistair. Eyeing up the strippers.'

'Maybe we ought to go up there.' Tom is so bloody transparent, but I don't care.

'Who's coming to help me get him the fuck away from this place? The police will be onto him in no time.' I look at Bart, who is already resigned to the fact he's going to have to traipse over to the farm with me, and then at Zoë, who isn't about to let her boyfriend go and gawp at naked women without being glued to his side.

Undeniably pleased with herself at the drama she's provoked, Charlotte offers to show us the way and we're about to head off when Amita wades in. 'Hang on a minute, blondie. Did you come all the way down here to tell Lou that?'

'Fuck no. Why would I do that? I saw Tom by complete coincidence five minutes ago – I only nipped in here to say hi to my boyfriend. He's the wedding DJ.' Typical. Some things never change.

It's only when Bart steps on the back of my flip-flop and trips me up ten minutes later that I realise I didn't say goodbye to Matt.

Seventeen

The farmhouse isn't on the festival site map. Friday night begins with a secret VIP party, completely unofficial, with a stream of helicopters dropping off celebs and bigwigs. Once the mix of models, musicians and money men slink back to their motorhomes or boutique country bolt-holes, the party continues. As the weekend progresses, the guests become gradually less glamorous and the entertainment dodgier.

It's the same every year. The party is just a front. While the police dogs over at the main entrance go crazy at teenage boys with small stashes of weed in their socks, this is where the lion's share of the drugs come in, on the choppers.

The security are expressionless meatheads. I have my Access All Areas pass at the ready but all they do is give Charlotte a nod and step aside. We duck as a helicopter comes down to land in a field.

The farmhouse itself is in darkness but flashing lights splinter through gaps in the walls of a huge barn that lies to the left of the farmhouse, and faint glows seep out elsewhere. The chopper blades are still rotating, covering everything in white noise, and I can only see Zoë scream when a chicken brushes past her leg.

Inside is the familiar stagnant thud of a dull, slouchy bass line, massaging people who have all been snorting coke for too long and haven't slept for days. Damp, heavy air and the smell of straw mix together to make a musty haze. The place is a claustrophobic maze of hay bale booths with stacks of pallets for tables. Topless waitresses in denim hot pants and Ugg boots are carrying trays of drinks out from a bar at the very back where the kind of east London strippers that give City blokes an eyeful for the price of a bottled lager any afternoon of the week are dancing on makeshift podiums made from industrial-sized wire-cable spools.

Charlotte's cold bloodless fingers lock tightly into mine. 'This way.'

I look back to check that Bart, Zoë and Tom are still jabbering along behind me, then in front again at Charlotte's stringy highlights and the silhouette of her cheekbones, raised with her smug smile. It's sickening, the pleasure she clearly gets from picking at the scabs on other people's relationships.

My heart races at the prospect of seeing Dan but it sinks again when Charlotte shoves me in front of him. He's glassy-eyed, hollow-cheeked, inhaling deeply through his nostrils. He has a gormless look on his face when he sees me, physically unable to register the surprise I know is jolting around the neural connectors in his brain. I've seen him in this state, countless times. I used to think he was a twisted, sexy mess.

Before I get the chance to pull him aside, Steve and Alistair cut across me to shake hands with Tom. They're followed by Gary, another member of their crew who's just come back out of the woodwork after four or five years in Australia. A mediocre West End hairdresser here, he bagged a senior stylist position in one of Sydney's most prestigious salons as well as a regular supply of session work at a string of glossy Aussie magazines. Typically, rather than grab the opportunity for all it was worth, he pissed it straight up the wall and eventually arrived back home with a nasty bump.

Now, well over a decade after he bought it, he's still wearing his old brown leather biker jacket, despite a rip in the sleeve, like the ghost of Glam House past. It belongs to a time when almost every club had a No Trainers policy and people wore their tacky-smart best.

His vacant gaze is re-energised momentarily into a

leer when it falls on Charlotte, but she's not having any of it and steers my husband and I towards each other. 'There. That's my good deed done for the day.'

Dan glares at her as hard as someone in his state can glare without it bottoming out into nothing and she's off, leeching around Steve and Alistair. Bart and Zoë are standing, heads tilted, arms crossed, up by the strippers, critiquing them like they're exhibits at Tate Modern.

Close up, the white wife-beater Dan's wearing is filthy and I can smell his sweat.

'The police are looking for you.'

He looks right at me. I think I can see vulnerability in his eyes and almost feel sorry for him, but it's probably just the drugs.

'It's safe. They won't set foot in the place. Everyone's on backhanders . . .' He seems pleased with himself and passes me a wrap.

'I don't want any, Dan. You're in serious trouble. That kid you whacked is on a life-support machine.' I'd been planning to persuade him to hand himself in but realise there isn't any point.

He starts going through the motions. 'It was an accident. I didn't mean for him to smash his nut on the floor like that.'

'What the hell are you talking about? He was already flat out on the floor when you started kicking him to

160

pieces. Dan, I saw you. Everybody saw you.' I'm exasperated and realise I've started to sound shrill, when I wanted to come across as calm and in control. My head hurts.

I can see his hackles start to rise. Tom has been watching what's brewing and steps in to try and smooth things over.

'Mate, what's up?'

'Nothing . . . All I did was give that little cunt what he was asking for. I thought he was going to hit me. Then he tripped.'

'I know, man. It'll all get sorted.'

Tom knows precisely how to operate Dan and any tension dissipates as quickly as it emerged with a few matey pats on the back: permission to stick his head back into the dingy cave he's hiding in.

Tom rubs my arm and smiles at me, glassy-eyed. He's seen it all before in one way or another. The trouble is, although it comes out of his uncomplicated and genuine desire for everyone to have a good time, all Tom is doing is papering over the cracks.

There's no point in any of us trying to have this conversation now: if Dan didn't run away with his tail between his legs last night there's no way he's going to leave now. We don't say another word, just go back over and join the others like nothing's happened.

A waitress brings over a trayful of beers. I don't really

want it but take one anyway, leaving a space that reveals a tennis-ball-shaped fake boob with a big shiny brown nipple. There's a sinking inevitability about this barn.

Bart's with Zoë talking bollocks to a sixty-something veteran showbiz reporter I recognise from the telly. She hasn't got round to leaving after last night and is dishevelled, in an elderly bourgeois way. Her spiked-up wiry jet-black hair is limp in places.

The rest of the guys stand in a semicircle, alternating head-nodding and zoning out with shuffling around in half-arsed schoolboy attempts to impress each other. Occasionally they glance at the naked women dancing in front of them. One of them has really bad in-growing hairs on her bikini line. Soon, though, the girls take a break, wrap themselves in satin dressing gowns and sit down with a drink a few hay bales away. Steve and Alistair head over to join them.

The whole scenario depresses me in a way that reminds me of a morning a month or so ago when I got out of bed to find Dan slouched on our sofa, snoring, one hand down his trousers, the other holding a cappuccino frother. On the table in front of him were an empty wrap, a credit card for a foreign bank I've never heard of and a copy of *Razzle*. I still have no idea what the cappuccino frother was all about – what could he have been using it for? – maybe Dan didn't really know either, but the coarseness of it all made me sad and weary.

Bart and Zoë drag their new friend over to park up on the straw next to me. I look at her ornate antique jewellery and thick black eyeliner. 'Who is she?' I ask Bart, while Zoë yaps away at her.

'I couldn't make out what she said ... I think she did an exposé on Mick Jagger in the sixties.'

'Thanks for coming with me, Bart.' I take hold of his hand. 'You knew it'd be a waste of time, didn't you?'

He doesn't hear. He's watching Al, who is hissing into one of the stripper's faces, holding her chin with one hand. Poor cow has probably just given him the brush-off or made an inoffensive remark to her friends about the funny-shaped, overpriced shoes he's got on.

Alistair's face is warped and twisted, sick with distaste for the redhead, but he's not stupid and doesn't draw attention to himself. He keeps his actions small, and when another of the other girls intervenes, he throws one more intimidating mouthful at both of them, gets up and leaves. Steve follows him, shaking his head but trying to suppress a grin nonetheless.

When they get back over to Tom and Dan, they're both laughing their heads off. Dan calls him a sick bastard – but not as a chastisement, more a token of spineless collusion – and Tom just looks down at his beer until they start talking about something else.

Hands up, I've been guilty of this perverted kind of honour among thieves. Everything excused because you were off your face. Normally post the event, midweek in the pub, laughing at the previous weekend's seventy-two-hour lapse in morality. But I'm sick of it. It's been so long since Dan and the others have had a rational thought, they've turned into a pack of dogs.

What's happened to everyone and at what point did I lose the ability to gauge what's been going on with my life? This arrogant, self-delusionary bullshit has been carrying on for years and years. It's shameful.

All the while I've been sneering at Gary with his crappy old leather jacket, I'm just as guilty, looking down from my high horse with the same bleached-blonde shoulder-length hair I've had for the last ten years. Crash and burn, crash and burn, crash and burn. Nothing much has changed bar the sinking expectations we have of ourselves and of each other. If we were simply turning into the sort of sad old caners as a teenager I'd see out and feel embarrassed for, that would be one thing, but Dan, this whole situation now, the guy in hospital, it's altogether more serious than that. I can't stay in this barn any longer.

'Who's coming back?' I make sure everyone hears over the music. 'I know you can't, Dan . . .' I don't extend my gaze to Steve and Alistair.

Bart and Zoë stand up and begin to say their good-byes to their new friend. Tom looks down at his beer again.

'Tom?' Zoë knows he's been sucked in. He's not an arsehole like the others, but he's still stuck to them like glue. 'Fine. Call me later.'

'We have to get back to the wedding we came to . . .' I say, but the boys aren't listening, engrossed in some pointless conversation or other. One of the strippers waves goodbye.

As the three of us head towards the door, the darkness and vulgarity begins to dwindle. Outside fresh, cool air greets us.

'Jesus. What was that all about? Let's get back to the cheesy wedding disco, away from the freaks.' I pull Bart and Zoë towards the lane we'd come up earlier with Charlotte, but Zoë's stopped in her tracks, frozen by what she's seen down the side of the barn.

At first it's a bit confusing. Something's off-kilter. There's a guy on his knees, head bobbing into the crotch of a tall girl leaning against the wooden wall.

'That's no woman, it's a bloke in a dress.' Bart's starting to put it all together. He's right. Then it hits me. It's Gary on his knees giving some old tranny head. I'd recognise that knackered brown leather jacket anywhere.

Eighteen

'Stop for a minute. I want to show you something.'

On the short walk along the lane, away from the cesspit up at the barn, Zoë has been unusually quiet. Back on the main site she pulls her phone out of the tiny tan leather bag that's hanging on a strap running from her right shoulder down to her left hip. She'd been fiddling with the buckle all the way down the lane. Now I know why.

'His name's Jonny . . .'

We all squash together, block the brightness from the floodlight we're underneath, and shift apart again so that we can all look at the face on the phone's screen properly.

He's right up close to the lens and it's a bit blurred.

Zoë steps back to give us some more light. She inhales really deeply with every breath and constantly rubs her left forearm with her right hand. Both Bart and I look at her blankly and straight back down at the phone.

The fleshy, stubbly profile that's playing at ignoring the camera held right up to it looks mid-twenties and is backlit by a fluorescence that's coming from a stage some distance behind. It looks like he's at a gig or something. He's got a serious art-school thing going on and, even with a slight double chin, has a candid appeal about him.

We both carry on staring down and Zoë chatters to the backs of our heads like she always does, but self-consciously. For once we hang on every word.

'He runs the studio at work.'

I haven't seen quite as much of Zoë as I used to and my head must have been so far up my own arse recently I didn't have an inkling that something out of the ordinary was going on.

While Tom sat in the same pubs, having the same old conversations with the same old faces, Jonny had picked Zoë up after work and driven to the seaside where they had fish and chips for tea. Another time they'd snuck off out of the office and wandered around London Zoo for the afternoon, spent the evening drinking in Soho and ended up in a tacky disco playing eighties music. She makes it clear they haven't had sex yet and her voice is defiant rather than defensive. Any reservations she may have had about what she'd been up to were ground up into dust back in the barn.

'Wow.' I don't know what else to say. I love Tom to pieces but my instant reaction is to congratulate, not discourage her.

It's odd. I've known Zoë for just about as long as I've been with Dan and although we regularly help ourselves to each other's clean knickers, make-up remover and tampons on a Sunday morning, rather than call it a day and go home, we hardly ever talk about anything more important: she knows how to talk me down from a panic attack or what to tell a medic if I need one, but I never really discuss why it happens in the first place. Instead, we rattle on about where we're going or where we've been. Who was there, what stupid thing they said or did, what some girl was wearing, what her problem was. We give everyone else a good going-over but never allow each other the same depth.

Bart play-punches Zoë's tiny fleshy arm. His mouth stretched into one big cheesy grin. 'You kept that one quiet.' He's never made a secret of the fact that he finds both of our men limited in their appeal. Zoë shrugs modestly.

'What are you going to do?' It feels weird to ask, especially when I know the answer already.

'What does it look like, Lou? Duh.' Bart is baffled that I'd even bother to ask.

Zoë takes one more look at the screen and puts it back in her little bag.

'He's here, now, with the guys from work ... He called earlier to see if I could sneak off.'

'What are you waiting for?' Bart doesn't get how girls need to edge into action sometimes, rather than jump.

'It's not as simple as that,' I say, assuming the ill-fitting hat of know-it-all mature, married woman.

Zoë met Tom shortly after she came to London, from Reading, about seven years ago and they've been together ever since.

'Actually, do you know what? It's not that complicated.' Zoë is still rubbing her arm but not as quickly. 'Tom's always looked after me. He's brilliant. But he'd be happy doing coke in the pub toilets and coming home to dance to his old Happy Mondays records in the front room with Dan all night, every night, for the rest of his life. Lou, you're older than me. You've been going along with all this for even longer. I don't know how you keep doing it.'

I'm genuinely happy for her but she's just made me feel like a complete loser. Still, she's right. Between the lot of us we've relegated the possibilities of the most highly charged city in the world to the same division as those in the small down-at-heel towns we'd left behind us.

'I might even want to go and work in New York for a year or something. I don't mean with Jonny particularly either.'

'Are you going to meet him now?' I'm panicked that I'll never see her again.

'No.' She gives me a clammy, pilled-up hug. 'At least not until I've rocked out to "My Sharona" with Heather's mum . . .'

Bart slaps us both on the back. 'I've kept saying you should come out with me more often.'

Nineteen

The first thing Dan ever said to me was: 'You're wasting your time.' He said the hand of cards I was holding was a flat-out disaster, nodded over to my editor's girl-friend Siobhan, and said, 'Tank it. She's about to piss all over you.'

It's impossible to think it was so long ago. It's as clear as if it were last week. We were at a poker night in a members' club in Soho. The press launch for a new jeans range. The PR company had given its favourite maga-zines a card dealer and eight seats in a room full of tables covered with green baize and litre bottles of vodka, whisky and gin. Dan was gatecrashing – he was supposed to be keeping his flatmate company by the decks in the corner while he played some records, but instead Dan spent most of the evening hopping between tables, making chit-chat, eyeing up cards and topping up his vodka.

Dan was in low-slung baggy blue jeans, chunky white sneakers and a navy windcheater done right up to his chin, even though we were inside and it was a mild May evening. There were soft pockets of low red light over each of the circular tables that filled the dark smoky room. Si, the DJ, was playing lazy, downtempo music, a few waitresses milled around with mini burger and mini fish-and-chip canapés. The rest of us, the guests, displayed varying degrees of card savvy.

My nose was out of joint: just before we'd left for the party Josh, my editor, had given his new girlfriend a bottle of perfume, a sample, that had been biked over earlier in the day to the office, addressed to me. 'Typical,' I said to Dan. 'She's already nabbed my Comme des Garçons perfume, now she's going to go home with three pairs of jeans as well. It's not fair, I need all the help I can bloody well get.'

Dan shrugged and smiled. 'You look all right to me.'

We were playing for chips that could be exchanged for clothes at the end of the party. Dan knew that but didn't understand why I was moaning about perfume. He told me afterwards that he just laughed along because he fancied me.

We made small talk. I told him I was the staff writer on *Pocket*, and that the lot around the table were the guys from the office. The kid next to me was Bart, with us on work experience and already shit-faced on neat Scotch.

I'd been on staff at *Pocket* for coming up to two years. I'd got the job after making myself as useful as was humanly possible for six months, working for free in the office and paying the rent with shifts in a pub for suits at night.

Pocket was a lifestyle mag for people who were savvy about art, design and fashion. We had 'experts' writing for each section of the magazine so I didn't get to do much real writing. The biggest thing I ever did was a double page on Heather Graham who'd just played Rollergirl in *Boogie Nights*. Mostly I did the snippets in the newsy front section which covered everything from a new bar opening to mini trend-spotting lists. Consequently I got invited absolutely everywhere and was sent loads of random goodies, like expensive perfume, every day.

When I asked Dan what he did he just said, 'Clubs.' Slightly arrogant and vague. I wondered if it was a prompt to ask more questions, or whether he sold drugs and it was a polite 'stop there'? He was far too handsome, I thought. Even if all the elements are there, something always gets in the way with those guys.

Dan had the same brutish jet-black skinhead he has now. It jars with his bone structure in a profound and beautiful way. Like so many of the contradictions he's made up of. Yet it wasn't simply the way that competing characteristics melded which made him so desirable.

Dan's not perfect-looking by any standard – his nose is kind of wonky and his teeth are big and yellow – but he has a magnetism that makes other people turn their heads and take notice. Physical presence that is disproportionate to his stature. It's not an over-powering onslaught of predictable sexual charisma, more a seeping of something, an essence, that makes people – like me, back then – want to listen to what he says, laugh, feel good and prickle with excitement whenever they have to lean in close to be heard in a noisy club.

I laid my cards down and bowed out, making myself fully available, but the moment I did Dan was up and off again, flitting around. I made a point of not looking bothered, rather tried to look busy instead and got up to squidge in next to my old friend Aurelie who'd arrived, late, on her magazine's table. By this time she was assistant art director on a recently launched rival to *Time Out*.

I asked Aurelie if she knew the guy with the DJ. She didn't but leant over to Bob, their overweight nightlife editor.

'It's Dan something.'

'Is he a promoter?' I asked Bob.

'More of a face, you know.'

I nodded. Who knows what half the people kicking around this town actually do to pay the rent. I once went for a drink with a guy who turned out to be an offal trader. The mystique of 'face' was much nicer.

'Actually, love, the last time I saw Dan he ran to the end of Brighton Pier and jumped straight in,' said Bob. 'DoggyDisco were doing a one-off night down there, think they'd even put some coaches on, and he had some bet on with Big Carlos. There you go, that's what he does. End-of-pier entertainment.'

'Why don't you go and ask him?' Aurelie was blunt as ever. 'Does anyone have a light?' She was chain-smoking Mayfair Lights and poking around in her handbag for some chewing gum.

I made a hamfisted job of looking popular and actively uninterested in 'Dan Something'. Turning my back when he was nearby, amid other flimsy teenage gestures. I struck up a pointless conversation with a Brazilian male model the PR company had hired to hang around looking gorgeous in the jeans they were promoting. He could hardly speak any English, got the wrong end of the stick and somehow thought I worked in the art department at *Elle*. He gave me his agency calling card, with a few photos of him on and his agency phone number, then tried to get me in the loos for a snog, mistaking me for someone who could help with his career.

After half an hour of ignoring Dan, in the hope that he would come back over and start talking to me again,

I gave up and sat down next to Bart who was trying his best to focus on his hand of cards. I picked up a couple from the floor that he'd dropped without realising. When I brought my head back up above the table, Dan was crouching down next to me, pouring some more vodka.

He gave me a killer smile and whispered into my ear. He asked me if I was up for a game of our own. If he did a bit of spying around the tables, how about splitting any clothes vouchers I won? All the clothes were giveaways so it wasn't stealing, just a bit cheeky. He stood up straight, put his hand on his hip and took a drag of his cigarette. 'You in?'

I couldn't be sure if he meant to kiss the side of my face or if it was just his lips brushing against it as he stood up. Of course I was in.

Twenty

When Dan said he worked in clubs it was shorthand for behind the bar, on the door or playing the records in any number of venues. It made no odds to me. I wasn't after a man to bring home the bacon, I wanted someone who could push my buttons.

Dan and I had fallen out of the pair of plain black doors from the club into the street, laughing our heads off, trying to breathe, each clutching a bag of clothes. I packed Bart off towards the night bus at Piccadilly Circus and, once he'd toddled off, I misjudged my stance and thudded back against a wall. Dan leant in and kissed me. As he did there was a bit of a splash by our feet. We stepped out of the puddle of tramp wee and carried on snogging further along the pavement.

We'd been kicked out, in the nicest of ways, after

I'd scooped up a gargantuan pile of chips inside my T-shirt, flopped down beside Aurelie and let them spill all over the table, interrupting another game that was going on.

My mountain of chips made quite an impact: the head of marketing was hammered too but had a ringside seat as the chips went flying. He'd had eyes in the back of his head all night – it was his event after all – and he soon put two and two together. We were pulled aside, and, at the same time as being reprimanded, were discreetly awarded for bringing some chutzpah to the party with some clothes. Then we were told, very nicely, it was probably time to leave.

Dan kissed me. His palms were firm on either side of my hips and his index fingers and thumbs pushed into the fat bits above the waistband of my jeans. I sometimes used to pinch the parts of me I'd rather there were less of, try to pull bits of the tops of my arms, my hips, my thighs out of view in front of the mirror in search of a skinny version of myself. Until then, with Dan, the penny dropped. I got it. I began to genuinely appreciate and understand the pleasures of my own flesh. It was a revelation.

I was twenty-five but it was the first time I'd felt like I was with a man, rather than someone who was still navigating the choppy passage from student to grown-up. It wasn't Dan's age, he's only a year older than me, rather it was that he was simply all man. A cliché, for sure, but that's how it was.

I'd played it safe with boyfriends in the past. I enjoyed the way they inevitably came to regard me as a bit of a handful and I played up to it. With Dan it all turned on its head. Everything he did was to the nth and life switched gears. I'd met my match, someone who loved the drama as much as I did. We had sex on the first night. We didn't ever do 'dates'. We were both out drinking and dancing almost every night and, depending on what was happening, we'd hook up somewhere along the line and share a cab home. Between us we could go anywhere: if I hadn't received an invite to a party off the back of the magazine, Dan would know someone to wave us in.

Without a proper job, I never quite knew when Dan was going to surface. So while I loved the unpredictability and the excitement that brought to the relationship, sometimes, on the quiet, I felt a bit short-changed.

For his birthday, four weeks after we met, I surprised him with a long weekend in Lisbon. We'd talked about going to Prague after just two or three days together, like people do when they're in that lusty, just-got-it-together state, but I was practically aching for sunshine. Holidays had been thin on the ground since I'd graduated and started paying my own way.

Having Dan to myself for four days, both of us on the same timeline, was an immense prospect, and the formality of checking through an airport made going away together feel like a big statement. The banality threw a new spin on us too. We were Dan and Louisa who'd spent half an hour trying to find a parking space at Stansted at five in the morning. My awesomely handsome new boyfriend, who flew around town all night, began to really feel like my real-time boyfriend, rather than a fiction.

The first two days in Lisbon passed as they would for any new couple who'd left town for a mini-break. It wasn't like we knew anyone in Lisbon. We sat at tables in the street drinking long, condensation-coated glasses of beer and had sex morning, noon and night in a crappy hotel room that was more like a cupboard. Not just any old cupboard either. Our room was next door to a gigantic air-con unit for the entire building, and at night its whirring and pulsating made our room even hotter than it was outside. It didn't matter. It just made the sex sweatier.

We'd spent practically every night together since we'd met but the contents of our travel bags were still unfamiliar to one another. We hadn't started using the same shampoo or toothpaste, and a couple of times, when he was in the shower, I took the opportunity to nose around in his holdall. I raised my eyebrows, endeared and amused by a couple of old paperbacks about conspiracy theories and some Armani sunglasses with metal-rimmed oblong frames that didn't look like they should belong to him.

On Sunday, day three of the mini-break, we caught a train down the coast. We bought a box of custard tarts and sat drinking Mateus rosé wine from the supermarket out of plastic cups at the end of a jetty, somewhere on the outskirts of Estoril. A few young kids came along and started diving and jumping into the water.

It wasn't the prettiest of spots but it was too hot to walk any further. There was a lot of concrete and not much beach, but there was iodine in the air, the sun was beating down and we'd got cheap wine to drink. We took the deep, nasal lugs of air you take when you haven't been near the ocean for a while. I looked over at Dan, who'd just taken his T-shirt off. I'd never had a seriously fit boyfriend before and it gave me a real kick.

I remembered the story Aurelie's workmate Bob, the clubs editor, had told me about, when Dan had launched himself off the pier in Brighton. I jumped to my feet, kicked off my flip-flops, yanked down my short jersey skirt, and dived in off the side of the jetty. I'd completely overlooked that we were beside the Atlantic and not the Med – even in the summer the water was bracing.

My chest contracted and I screamed, hysterically, a combination of exuberance and shock.

The young kids messing around in the water were gobsmacked. For once their volume went down to zero. I was for all intents and purposes an adult, even worse a tourist, who had dived into the sea in her knickers and a vest. Dan looked down at me, took off his funny rectangular sunglasses and, with less than his usual grace, stacked his dive and bellyflopped in.

Around midnight, back in Lisbon, we pulled our twin mattresses out onto the narrow balcony of our hotel room and lay there talking into the night. The sounds from the streets below filtered up and we took it in turns to tell each other, properly, for the first time in real detail about our families, old boyfriends and girlfriends, past holidays. None of it was sensational – both of us were actually quite boring, on paper – but we were filling in the gaps with all the stuff that helped to make more sense of the two people who'd met back in London.

After we threw our bags back down on the floor of my flat on Monday night we polished off the one last bottle of rosé wine from the supermarket in Lisbon and messed around recording a joint answerphone message on the machine in the lounge.

Dan moved in with just one carload of stuff from the place he shared in Dalston. My red Golf, proud and shiny back then, packed with a few suitcases of clothes, six crates of records, a dustbin bag of books and a box of flyers and fanzines he'd collected from way back.

Twenty-one

The reception is in full swing and I'm determined to prove to my friends that, minus my husband, I can get through a night out without any drama. After Zoë's revelation about her new guy I feel even less guilty about walking away and leaving Dan to flounder in his own sewer. I've wasted enough time trying to save him. It's sad that this is where we've got to, but it's stopping right here.

The others neck more of Tom's pills. Zoë had helped herself from the bag in his pocket before leaving the barn. I stick with vodka tonic and a small line of coke left over from last night. It's a reluctant precaution but there's no way I can risk getting shit-faced again. My plan is a few more hours here then I'm turning in.

None of us are quite ready to step back onto the dance floor, so we stand at the edge, heads nodding to

Bon Jovi, scoring air guitarists out of ten. A gang of small kids copy the receptionist from Felipe's work as she does a knee-drop guitar-hero move. Luckily they're behind so they're not treated to the flash of lacy crotch we get. Nelson puts another drink in everyone's hand and says they've got karaoke going on in the yurt. No one, it seems, has marquees any more.

We squeeze in at the back of the billowing tent. It's hot and noisy but cushion-strewn, dimly lit and cosy. A guy and a girl are doing 'Rhinestone Cowboy', but I can't see who they are. A yurt's worth of hoarse voices joins in. Helena and Nelson push through to the front, nudging hello to the new friends they'd made in here while we'd been off rubbing shoulders with the dregs.

I hang back until I see the others pick up bottles of vodka from a low table in the middle and top up their drinks. In for a penny, in for a pound. Dan's not ruining this for me.

Nelson and Helena muscle straight in and join their new best friends up the front for a Cher-off to 'Gypsies, Tramps and Thieves'. Bart and Zoë are flicking through the songbook like a pair of overexcited hairdressers on a hen night. I rack my brains for something cool and ironic for when the inevitable comes around. All I can think of is 'Morning Train (9 to 5)' by Sheena Easton, but that's no good because half the people here, including Bart, won't have heard of it, and I'll look ancient. Or maybe it could work. When Marcus, Heather's brother, launches into 'We Don't Have To Take Our Clothes Off', Bart yanks me up onto the table in the middle, sending bottles flying, to join him in a dance routine he must have memorised from *Top of the Pops* aged five.

Somehow, thank goodness, my appalling taste in men doesn't extend to Bart. He's an absolute diamond. Nights out with him end in silliness; one of the very first times we went out we slept on the office floor in two rolled-up carpets. I only wish that when he laughs and asks why I put up with my husband carrying on like a wanker, he's having a joke with me. Instead I've started to see what he means.

Now we're on the table, everyone wants to get on it. All stooping, bums and elbows nudging back and forth, our heads making shapes in the tent fabric. Some guy gets his watch strap caught in the tassles from my dress while Melanie, Felipe's office manager, quickly sweeps the remaining vodka bottles from the table into her arms and into safety, minus the one Bart has looted, swigs from and passes around.

Before long we're hot and sweaty and have sore throats, like everyone else. Heather and Felipe crowd-surf to the front for a slurred rendition of 'Love Is in the Air' and the place erupts: 'La la la, La la la. Love Is in the Air.'

I'm jealous when I look around at my friends, coming up on their pills, but I'm in a pretty good place myself. I step down, pick up the songbook from the floor and hurriedly look for one I can make Bart do with me. I rock from side to side to the music, still only at artists beginning with B.

'Bruce Springsteen could work . . . Sorry, did I spit in your ear?'

It's Matt, bending down next to me. Bright-red-faced, wide-eyed, wiping his mouth. I fight the urge to rub my ear and pretend he didn't cover it in saliva. '"Born to Run". It's got to be, hasn't it?'

I shake my head. Panic shoots through me at the thought of singing in front of him, and I screw my nose up at his suggestion. He looks like he's walked through a giant humidifier while I feel drips of perspiration run down my back, bouncing off the man-made fibres of the dress he'd help me find. I carry on turning pages, quicker now so he can't pin me down to anything else.

He leans into my ear again and I move back, scared he'll gob in it again. I can't hear what he said. He tries again. This time I hear.

'Where've you been?'

'You don't want to know . . .' I say.

I look closer into the book but realise I'm being a jerk, so turn, smile right at him and raise my hands, shake my head. 'It's a long story.'

Before he gets the chance to ask any more, one of his mates taps him on the shoulder and nods upwards at the change in music.

'Shit, it's me . . .'

I watch as he bends the whole of his right side into the mike and starts stirring up the first few lines of an old Elvis song, 'If I Can Dream'. It's a big gospel track and the hollow karaoke backing music hardly holds it up, but Matt's got a pretty good Elvis rasp and he really goes for it as the song builds up to a belting crescendo. The way he manages quite skilfully to offset the evangelism of the song's lyric with some Las Vegas-era mike swinging is pretty impressive. So much so that I become a tiny bit misty-eyed and for a split second almost forget that Elvis croaked on the toilet and I – whatever I think of Dan right now – have a husband. Eventually someone gives Matt a dry-ice finale courtesy of the mini fire extinguisher and he completely disappears.

'Who's the guy?' It's Bart now. 'You're all at it, aren't you?'

'No one. He's a friend of Heather's. Don't you think I've got enough on my plate right now?' By the time I finish slapping Bart, Matt's back and we give him another round of applause.

'Anyone want to come outside for a fag?'

'Don't smoke, mate,' Bart lies, looking straight at me.

It's not cold outside but I shiver, skin covered in dry sweat, as Matt lights my cigarette. I inhale deeply, hear my phone ring and pull it out of my bag. Not only have I been racking up missed calls all day, both from Alexa and the PR of the band I should have interviewed, but Andrew Glass has been leaving messages too. The only plan I've been able to concoct is to stick my head in the sand and face the music, a whole bloody orchestra's worth, back in the office on Monday.

'Shit.' My voice wavers with the quickening of my pulse.

'Is it your fella?' Matt sits down on a tree stump, vacating my periphery.

'No . . . It's my mum.'

Something's wrong. I pick up.

'Louisa love, I got you, thank goodness. You mustn't worry but it's your dad . . .'

I listen helplessly to what she has to say. Heart thumping, eyes burning, crouched down, looking at my dirty feet. I stand up, pace about and crouch down again. She tells me that there's no point coming home right now. I ask her to call me as soon as there's an update and hang up.

'What's happening? Are you OK?' Matt gets up and stretches an arm out towards me.

'It's my dad. He went out with the dog this morning and hasn't come home. The police are looking for him . . .'

I hadn't spoke to my mum in weeks. I'd not returned any calls and so she didn't know I was out of town this weekend.

My throat is clogged up and I can hardly get any words out. Matt rubs my back. 'She was calling to make sure she spoke to me before I heard anything ... The police are considering putting a description of him on air – local radio stations and the south-east news. They're worried about what state he might be in.'

Twenty-two

I can barely say the word. My dad has Alzheimer's. I never talk about it. He's been off work for a few years now. First the doctors thought it was depression. I remember hoping it was a brain tumour. Anything but the hopeless diagnosis we knew was coming. I'd been with him and my mum at the hospital when they sat us down and told us his brain scans were reflective of someone in the early stages of the disease. I cried. My mum gave me a hug and my dad sat there quietly before they took him off to have some more tests done.

The thing about London, about the kind of work I do, the kind of people I hang out with, is that no one expects you to tell them anything about yourself. Not really. Which suits me. I'm eaten up when I see other families, several generations deep, out enjoying them-selves in a restaurant headed up by a dominant, wine-list-wielding father. My dad is a small, confused grey-bearded man following my mum around, head down, hands in his pockets.

Something like this was bound to happen sooner or later. My brother is out looking. With today's heat everyone is worried that Dad has become dehydrated and disorientated. He forgets he needs to eat or drink sometimes.

I stand up, pull at my hair. My head feels like it's full of helium. I stagger around as each route out of this place turns into a dead end. It's almost midnight. The trains will have stopped, a cab – if I could find one – would require more cash than I have in my already pitifully overdrawn account, and even I know I'm in no state to drive.

I hear myself whimper at the thought of my dad scared, confused and the butt of jokes and teasing by the nasty little oiks that spill onto the streets at kicking-out time in the shitty little Kent town where I grew up, and where the rest of my family still live.

He has no control over the dog either. As the circuit board inside his brain continues to break down he tells her one thing when he means another. Now that communicating with people is increasingly reduced to a stuttering, repetitive and belittling experience, the simple connection Dad has with the daft, adoring spaniel has transformed into a refuge for him. If anything has happened to her, he will be beside himself. I become convinced she's got run over and he's been knocked down too, trying to rescue her. Or his coordination has given out on him, he's lost his footing and is lying unconscious at the edge of one of the small lakes just outside of town where boys with bum fluff and gold jewellery go to get stoned. I bend over, hug my ribs tighter and tighter, with each scenario.

Matt puts his arm around my shoulders and straightens me up. 'You can't do anything. Not at this time of night. Nothing terrible has happened. They would have found him by now. You'll have to wait till the morning.'

Wrenched back up, I try to look beyond him and glare into the disco lights flashing in the distance. Inviting them to hypnotise me.

He stands firm, but I break off from him as the utter fear of what could ultimately have happened rises in my throat and, for the second time today, I vomit.

The shock of puking at Matt's feet brings me back round to my senses. It's made him back off too. I look straight at him now. Eyes connecting with his, bile fizzing on my tongue.

He sidesteps the sick, pulls me into him and pushes my face into his shoulder. I'm sure I've smeared remnants of it onto his shirt now. He's unfazed. 'It's OK.' He taps my head. 'What the hell's going on in there?'

I push my head further into his shoulder and shake it slowly. My pulse has started to calm down and the black cotton in front of me has taken on a sharper, more tangible form. I can almost pick out the fibres as they weave into one another.

He tries again. 'Do you want me to go and get your friends? I don't mind . . .'

My entire body tenses up again and I shake my head, furiously this time.

'Fair enough, but let's move around a bit then. Come on.'

I pull my head up and we start walking. Away from the electronic sax solo halfway through the karaoke version of 'Fame' that's playing, and away from the rows of tea lights suspended on wires scoping out the perimeter of the hired wedding-field space.

I hold my phone tightly, checking it every thirty seconds or so, and I make sure I leave a good distance between myself and Matt as he surveys the line of falafel, smoothie and crêpe vendors. They're next to a small bar on the first, narrow stretch of the main site, before it opens out into a smoky, floodlit vista punctuated in the first instance by stilt walkers, glow sticks and underage girls. I let out a little yelp, struck by a bolt of ambiguous panic into my core. Matt doesn't seem to have heard. He heads over to the picnic tables to our left and I follow.

'Can I get you anything?' He shakes his pockets for coins.

I could do with a bottle of sparkling water to freshen my mouth up, and probably a beer too, if he's getting one for himself.

I stare down at weather-beaten grey wood until he's back. It's unnerving to be sat in front of someone who has garnered such an unpleasant, dramatic and unwelcome insight into my life in such an incredibly short time.

'Do you want me to help you find your husband?'

I look at Matt like he's crazy.

We sit in silence for a while. Me staring into my phone while Matt picks at something that isn't there on the table. I hardly know him and he's stuck out here with me while the rest of his mates are back at the reception.

'You don't have to stay with me now. I'll sort something out. I'll be fine.' I try to sound convincing.

'Are you nuts? You can't stay on your own when all this is going on. The wedding can survive without me ripping another Elvis classic to shreds.'

'I can't believe this is happening.'

'If you just want to hang out and wait for some news, that's completely cool.'

I can tell Matt means it. Beyond the long eyelashes, his eyes are straight up, honest. The one on the right side is just a tiny bit sleepy.

Every time I have to talk about my dad, it's like being at an AA meeting for the first time, confessing, exposing myself to feelings I'd rather not have to deal with or simply acknowledge.

'He's only late fifties ... He's never gone missing before.'

Matt shakes his head in sympathy and tells me not to be embarrassed but I am. Of myself. Not Dad. What Matt saw was a relatively minor freak-out. Sometimes, when I've got a really bad comedown and I'm lying in bed, I lose it so badly I slam my head against the pillow, hyperventilate, choke, bite the mattress and coerce Dan into having frantic, empty sex that grinds to a halt within seconds.

The screen of my phone flickers momentarily as another minute passes. 'This is torture, stranded here. This weekend's been a complete disaster ... Not that any of the other shit really matters now.'

Matt gives me a curious look. He can't resist the opportunity to pry a little, and let's face it, the guy deserves some kind of explanation after coming to my rescue, twice, and being puked on in the space of a few hours. So I give Matt a rundown of the past twenty-four hours, supported with some background information on my hedonistic template for married life and my complete inability to do anything but disappoint or infuriate my boss. As I keep on talking, my matter-of-factness about the whole shebang begins to trouble me. Christ knows what the stranger in front of me must be thinking.

Eventually I stop, look at my phone. More than ten minutes has disappeared.

'You'll sort it out. You seem like a smart girl.'

'I know exactly what I am.' I want everything to change.

'Honestly. You're not as messed up as you think you are. Your dad's sick and your husband, I'm sorry, but he just sounds like an arsehole.'

Matt's missed out the work debacle. With everything else that's going on it's easy to let that one slip through and I shouldn't have bothered reminding him.

'You'll get another job,' he says casually. 'Surely you're a bit too old to be dicking around with that style-mag nonsense anyway?'

Twenty-three

The jazz lounge is Matt's idea. He thinks it might be a good place to sit it out. Mellower, less people coming at you, some chairs and tables. Tangled up in knots I'd resisted, preferring to stay on the move, but the sickly-sweet smell of crêpes and teenage gurners outside eventually got the better of me.

Matt's talking about the young New York-based indie jazz group that are playing. He'd downloaded some of their stuff from a website I've never heard of and had read they'd be on here from midnight. I was right. He's a complete music nerd. Soon he's going to ask me if I was into the Smiths at school and I'm going to blow it by admitting I hate Morrissey.

We sit in the dimly lit tent and chain-smoke at one of its small tables that are draped with deep red velvet and topped with a small, red-bulbed fringed lampshade.

If I were feeling churlish I'd slag it off as a hazier, seedier version of *Later . . . with Jools Holland*, with grass underfoot as opposed to a hard studio floor. I'm not though. The band's gloopy noodling is soothing. An escape from the bass bin outside.

I'm exhausted. Insanely tired but wired with worry. I lean forward onto my elbows, tip my head downwards, yawn and walk my fingers up and down the back of my neck.

'I know what you mean.' Matt lets out a little yawn too. 'I'm usually crashed out on the sofa polishing off my second bottle of dessert wine and halfway through a double bill of movies by now.'

I sit listening to him as he runs through a regular weekend in Camden, making a valiant attempt to keep my mind off other things. He says that, without fail, he switches his phone off when he comes to and shuffles through the usual Saturday-morning hangover by stocking up on groceries on Parkway. Then he goes over to the offie for several small bottles of expensive sweet wine and finally to Virgin for an armload of DVDs. He makes his way back to his flat and doesn't leave until the next lunchtime, when he picks up the Sundays and plots up in the pub across the street from his place. He switches his phone back on first thing Monday morning when he gets into work.

'Don't you ever go out?'

'Yeah, but not really at the weekends.' He leans back to avoid the smoke he's just exhaled and leans back in again. 'Don't tell anyone but I've been inadvertently limbering up for that Elvis number all week. You know the Karaoke Box on Frith Street? I've been in there almost every night till God knows when, pissed up, banging a tambourine with the girls from work. It's got embarrassing.'

I smile and twist my mobile around and around in my palm, waiting to pounce when it vibrates. Matt carries on.

'Sometimes I'll meet up with my mate Ben and we'll go skating Saturday afternoon.'

Someone his age clunking around on a skateboard isn't right. I ask him what his girlfriend does while he's hanging around the South Bank with a load of spotty teenage skater boys.

'We broke up. The whole thing's a pain in the arse. I'm never going to another dinner party again. People only go to dinner parties at our age when they're in really shit relationships, don't they?'

'I don't go to dinner parties . . . but I am in a shit relationship.' I allow myself a small smile at my new self-awareness and at the ridiculous notion of going to dinner at one of our friends' houses with Dan.

'Don't tell me you haven't had to sit in someone's poky conversion flat while they've wheeled out the obscure vegetables and cuts of meat from Borough Market they've blown a week's wages on?'

I shake my head and laugh. 'I once saw a man pay five quid for two potatoes in Borough Market. No lie.' What was wrong with people?

'And after dinner everyone does too much coke and talks about their lives,' he adds. 'Then they go home and argue about who did too many drugs.'

We both laugh and I sigh; my thoughts switch back again to my dad. Matt is funny and I know exactly what he means but I can't think of anything else interesting to say and drift inwards. All I can think of is where my dad might be.

Matt pats the table decisively and says he's going to get us both a glass of red wine. The band starts to shake out its version of 'My Favourite Things' from *The Sound of Music*.

I watch a group of quiffed, thirty-something guys playing cards while one of the percussionists from the band snakes around the tables at the front, clapping, encouraging them to break into the brief ripples of applause you hear when live jazz is on the radio.

I stare at a girl dancing on her own at the side of the stage, making shapes like the silhouetted figure in the titles from *Tales of the Unexpected*, rhythmic and soft. I fix my gaze on her, and then it's suspended into nowhere, propped up by the music.

'I want the Coltrane version of this played at my funeral,' Matt says, the cigarette between his lips bobbing around as he leans over the lamp. He puts a glass in front of me. I shield my drink from the ash that's falling and look away, let down by the tactlessness of his remark.

He sets his glass down, takes his seat. 'I love the song is what I meant to say . . . How are you feeling?'

'Calmer. Definitely.'

'Good. What were we talking about before anyway?'

'Your crazy ex.' It slipped out.

He raises his eyes to the ceiling. 'Did we get to the crazy bit?'

I backtrack. 'When did you split up?'

'February. I should have jacked it in a year before that but she kept persuading me to give it another go. She still keeps calling me. Even now.'

'Fucking hell, we're all as bad as each other, aren't we?' I say, laughing at how ridiculous my own set-up has become. 'Going round in bloody circles. What is it? It didn't work the last six times we gave it another try, but because it was an absolute riot for the first eighteen months here we are, five years on, fresh start number seven.'

'I reckon I spent almost five grand on all that nonsense in the last stretch with her. We went on holiday for three weeks, clean slate and all that bollocks, but it was hopeless. She kept on trying to talk through stuff we'd been through a million times before or instigate sex, and there was no way that was on the cards, so I got stoned on the beach every day. Then she got the hump because I was stoned every day.'

I ask Matt when he thinks you finally get to the point that you know you genuinely don't give enough of a shit to try again and he tells me about the time when he came home at ten in the morning after a party to find both his girlfriend and her mother waiting for him in the living room. 'She got her mum to come over, because she didn't know what to do when I hadn't come back by five.'

'Christ, my mum would be over at mine a couple of times a week,' I say.

'Exactly. She knew I was at a party, what did she think I was doing?'

I play at interrogating him. 'All it takes is a phone call. What were you doing out all that time?'

Matt looks down at his fag and up at me. Uh-oh. 'Shagging some girl on the sofa after the party . . .'

'I didn't want to know that . . .'

We both look ahead at the band, embarrassed. Me in my evening dress and him with his neat side parting and top button done up. I let myself feel the music and, saying nothing, sink into it for a while until Matt jerks his chair backwards to stand, shake the hand and bear-hug a blond, freckly guy with a small tash wearing simple neutral cotton shorts and a short-sleeved shirt. It's got the same unfamilar little red label that Matt's shirt has on the pocket.

There's a pretty, friendly-faced woman beside him in a cute smock dress. Matt gives her a hug and a kiss on the cheek too. 'They said you were down here. I'm just taking a breather from that wedding . . . karaoke central. What's happening?'

The blond guy crosses his arms. 'We've lost our new Swedish directors. Twins. Lottie and me were having a scout around for them. Someone said they were off their tits talking into the tablecloths in here.'

Matt guffaws and the Essex boy is out of the can again. 'We've been in here about three-quarters of an hour. Haven't spotted them, mate.' He looks over at me and remembers his manners. 'Oh, this is Louisa . . . Louisa, Bruce and Lottie.'

I open my left hand into a wave and smile at them. Both smile back, and it's plain they think Matt's either pulled at the wedding or been rumbled with a new girlfriend he hasn't yet wheeled out in public.

'Can I get you guys a drink?' Bruce nods at our near-empty glasses and Matt raises his. 'Nice one. Red wine, Brucie.'

'Wine? Here? You're brave. Same for you, Louisa?'

I look over at Matt. 'Only if she drinks it slowly,' he

says. I could take this as patronising but I guess it's only because he's looking out for me. I do need to drink more slowly.

Lottie prods Matt in the ribs – 'Bloody cheek' – and follows Bruce over to the bar.

'Sorry. Is that OK? We can make our excuses if it's too much.'

It's fine. They seem nice, I say.

'They have me over for dinner sometimes in the week. Make sure I eat properly.'

They're nice people. Warm-spirited, funny and relaxed because they've left the kids in their tent with their new Polish nanny. Only thing is, with all the talk of missing Swedes and Bruce quizzing Matt about a planned move to the Ellis New York office, I feel like the Little Englander.

Lottie tells me she's a stay-at-home mum, but the satisfaction and affection with which she talks about family life in Belsize Park serves to make it equally as foreign and exotic to me as a new life in Manhattan.

'Anyway . . . enough about me. You and Matt, what's the story?' she asks far enough into the conversation to have made it onto the right side of polite, while the two men are talking about a snowboarding trip they're planning for later in the year.

'Oh, no, nothing like that. We just met at the wedding.' I wonder whether I should say I'm married, for emphasis, but decide it would actually sound more like I was protesting innocence. 'I got a bit too drunk, a bit too quickly, at the reception.' I go on to tell her that I fell into a lake and Matt helped sober me up. I've given up fronting. 'That sounds awful, doesn't it?'

She chinks her plastic glass against mine. 'That's what weddings are for.'

Phone vibrations tickle the table and I scoop up my Nokia, but it's still. Bruce starts talking into his handset.

My teeth knock gently against each other and Matt leans round the table, puts his hand over mine. 'OK?'

I tap my fingers on the tabletop, give him a little nod and dig out a firm 'Yes'. He winks in support.

Twenty-four

I pull the neck of the oversized sweatshirt I've borrowed from Lottie up over my nose and smell fabric conditioner. I sit and listen to her talking and imagine what it must be like to waft around all day, every day, like this.

We'd all left the jazz tent together to make our way back to the Boutique Field where Bruce, Lottie and their crowd are staying in the giant wigwams, a stone's throw from my tent. Everything in my bag is probably damp and musty by now so I tell Lottie I've forgotten to bring anything with sleeves.

Inside their tepee, she and I tiptoe over to peek at her beautiful, blond, curly-haired kids, out for the count in black-and-white animal-print sleeping bags. Next to them, the young Polish nanny is snoring. Matt and Bruce stand and fiddle with kids' toys amid empty wine bottles, Waitrose Save the Planet carriers and tiny Birkenstocks directly on the grass outside.

Soon though we're all camped out around a huge fire. The Swedish directing duo Bruce is looking after have resurfaced and are trying to scale the sushi stand that is boarded up for the night. I look down at my knees and wonder how the hell I'm going to get the grass stains off. Then I look at my phone. It's quarter to two. The heat from the fire pushes against my face and the flames dance around. I hope Dad's not cold.

Somehow, though, rather than feeling completely isolated and overwhelmed with worry, as I sit smoking my last few menthol cigarettes, I've become more composed, more philosophical about crossing off the hours until I'm fit to drive. There's nothing I can do but wait.

Someone called Toby is staying in the tepee next door. He's over by the sushi stand, a white square wooden box covered in black Japanese letters and padlocks, watching that the Swedes don't maim themselves ahead of a round of important appointments in London next week. Beth, Toby's wife, is bringing out armfuls of cushions and blankets for everyone while Lottie fills me in.

Toby was best man at their wedding. He and Beth live in Broxbourne, the Hertfordshire commuter town where they all grew up. They're all here on a jolly; both tepees came courtesy of the mobile phone network Toby works for.

Beth, who works in HR in the City, eventually squidges in between Lottie and Bruce, to my right. She's just put on some slouchy yoga pants underneath her fine long-sleeved cotton T-shirt dress. Her bobbed curly hair is shiny chocolate brown. She rubs moisturiser into her clean freckly face, neck and down into her cleavage as she talks about the fortnight she and Toby have just spent in Costa Rica.

'The guys where we were staying lit a fire for us on the beach one night. It was bliss, until I woke up the next day.'

She pulls up her right trouser leg and points to an ankle bracelet of pink mosquito bites, scabbed over.

'Stop trying to make out you're one of those earthy, get-back-to-nature types,' teases Lottie. 'Toby told me that your team of servants propped you up on a cabana and surrounded you with ice buckets, but you both got pissed and woke up at dawn bitten to pieces.'

Both women laugh while I picture Toby and Beth drinking cocktails in their swimsuits at one of those long-haul honeymoon resorts.

Beth's shins are shiny, smooth and tanned. Her toes are painted pillar-box red with a glossy clear top coat. The cuticles and shape of each nail are neat and tidy. The circle of broken skin looks like a complete aberration.

She helps herself to the joint in Bruce's hand and

waves it around, gesturing outwards. 'Yeah, well, it wasn't quite *Conde Nast Traveller*, but we had a great time.'

At first Beth comes across as all suburban, professional-couple affluence. But cut the crap and the kitchen full of Smeg appliances and she also has a no-shit attitude that cancels it out. I very consciously pull the plug on my auto-bitch the minute I start contrasting her appetite for five-star ostentation with Lottie's stealthier, classier, urban sophistication. Where did I get off?

It grates, but the reason Beth started to rub me up the wrong way is because she and I are not actually that different. It's written all over her. Small-town girl, parents guaranteed to have voted for Maggie in the eighties, probably packed her off for a few elocution lessons as a kid. It takes one to know one. I sense she wants people to notice the BMW key fob and the red soles of her Christian Louboutin flip-flops, just as I like to come across as cool and in the know.

I really like both women. Lottie and Beth are very close, old friends. Maybe I'd be a bit more lenient of all our differences and less envious of their friendship if I deigned to hang out with my old mates back home a bit more. I hardly see Amy these days. I'd dropped presents in for her kids at Christmas but that was it.

She and Dan had a blazing row on the way home from the wedding of another old mate last summer. He was off his head and had been plying Amy's husband Dave with coke all night. Then Dan trod mud all over the cream interior of her car. Heavily pregnant at the time and behind the wheel, she told Dan he was a jumped-up arsehole and made him walk the last few miles back to my mum and dad's. We spoke the next day – it would have been too weird if we hadn't – but besides Christmas that's been about it.

I start to feel very aware of what this lot here might be making of me.

'Michaela's caught some quality action today,' says Beth. 'Nutters.'

She forgets herself and shrieks out into the darkness for Michaela. Whoever Michaela is. She gets up for a look around when she gets no response.

'Who's Michaela?' I ask Lottie. I dread to think what she'd caught sight of.

'She's married to Joe. With the crew cut over there.'

I look over around Matt to my left at Joe who's close to horizontal. Baby-faced, olive skin, stubbly with a Greek look about him. He croaks hi to me, apologises for Matt's rudeness and lack of introductions, but his eyes are half closed and he looks like he's about to keel over. Matt rubs my arm and asks if I'm still OK. I tell him I am, that all the chat is helping to distract me from worrying.

Joe's been drinking all day while Michaela's working.

It's her big break as documentary-maker and she's directing her first BBC commission, all about festival culture.

Lottie carries on, describing in detail the furniture-restoration business Joe's building up from a workshop round the corner from their flat in Stoke Newington. She mentions styles and finishes I've never heard of. Most of my stuff is from Ikea. I've always been into going out and having a good time rather than creating a beautiful home; I'm the only person I know who didn't bother with a wedding list. I don't really give a toss about all that. Although maybe it is a bit shameful for a woman of my age to still be living with so much cheap flat-packed rubbish.

I'm saved from admitting to my shabby student decor when Beth reappears dragging a willowy and exhausted-looking woman, laden with camera bags. This must be Michaela. She takes one look at her husband and flops down behind us.

I smile a small hello and nudge Matt to budge up. He pushes Joe, who lumbers along a bit and passes out. Unlike the rest of Matt's friends, Michaela is north London liberal, born and bred. Dark shoulder-length hair pulled up into a ponytail and small hazel eyes. You can spot them a mile off. In a simple white vest top, stone-coloured drawstring trousers and Birkenstocks there's nothing frilly or showy about her.

She tells me she's 'looking at the festival environment as a unique, temporary micro society and is hoping to present a colourful twenty-first-century tangle of social strata, to try to give some insights into why now twelve million people in the UK alone will go to a festival this year'.

She wants her film to show what the experience means for different people. I'm impressed, jealous even. I'm an absolute tit for not taking my own career as seriously.

I'm slightly mortified when Matt announces: 'Louisa writes for *Neon*, you know?'

Michaela's documentary sounds anthropological. I'm incredibly aware that she's so much more articulate than I am and start to feel even shoddier about the band I didn't interview, Alexa and the *Neon* website.

'It's just a little magazine,' I say with false modesty, trying to remain upbeat in front of this group of strangers. I've used the line so many times when batting away compliments, but when I look at her for some recognition, there's none. Why would she know about *Neon*? Michaela's got bigger, prime-time-TV fish to fry.

In fact, why would any of the women I'm sat with here give a monkey's about what I do? I'm sure I would have pompously written them off in some pathetic way or other had we all gone to the same school, but now I find myself craving the way they're so happy in their own skins and fulfilling serious adult ambitions. I've had it with all the bullshit. I totally admire what they're doing with their lives.

One of my favourite pieces of TV ever was a documentary about Brockwell Park Lido. It must have gone on air about eight years ago. 'Do you know it?' I ask Michaela, changing the subject and switching gears. Of course she does.

It's all about the cross section of south London 'tribes' who cram around the open-air pool over the course of a summer, semi-naked, jostling for space. 'It makes me think of Salinas Beach in Ibiza. You know, how you start at one end with all the families making sandcastles and as you walk along it becomes pervier and pervier? You get right up the other end and there's the Muscle Marys with their cocks pierced,' I say.

Everyone laughs. Michaela has only been to Ibiza Yoga once, for a bikram boot camp, and in reality, it has been a few years since my last disaster-stricken week on the island with Dan but, she quickly admits, she's got more than her fair share of naked flesh tonight.

Beth and Lottie, who began chattering among themselves the minute they heard the word 'anthropological', shut up and turn round. Matt props his head on my shoulder too.

'. . . cliché of clichés. In the sauna,' says Michaela airily, noting the sudden rise in audience figures.

Every year, there are stories about the twenty-four-hour, nude sauna in the Star Children's Field, but I've never met anyone who's admitted to going further than feeling uncomfortable with the heat and leaving after just a little while. I'm curious.

Michaela starts to describe what happened, but quickly becomes exasperated with all the questions Lottie and Beth are firing at her. 'Just let me tell you what happened, OK? I can't hear myself think.'

She's been filming day and night and all anyone's interested in are the rude bits. Order in the classroom is quickly restored and Michaela continues. 'What's interesting is that it was a bunch of regular kids.'

The girls, Chloë and Jenny, both eighteen, from the West Country, were unremarkable and sat on white wipe-down cubes. Chloë's corkscrew black curls were pushed back off her face with an Alice band, her pale skin broken up with the odd pink acne scar. Jenny looked like she wore glasses but had taken them off. She had a mousy, bowl haircut framing a face with features too weak to support it, exaggerated by the smallness of her eyes. Both had their legs crossed but sat upright, nipples warm and flat, breasts shining with perspiration. Neither of the girls were used to the levels of attention they were getting.

Lined up opposite were Ryan, Lee and Darren. Three squaddies, all just nudging twenty, based in East Anglia.

Coarse and muscular, with the unique, homoerotic military disposition that puts soldiers at ease with each other's nudity. The five had been drinking and dropping pills together since they'd met earlier in the evening.

Michaela looks across at her husband, checking he's asleep. 'We had to go starkers too. My assistant David only started with me about a month ago.'

She'd kept them chatting and gradually they'd started talking more confidently into the camera and showing off. Only someone like Michaela, with urbane liberalism in her bones, could sincerely negate any fruitiness.

Whereas anyone else would say they could tell everyone was bang up for it, she says: 'What I felt was a primal appetite for adventure in these average kids. That's what I wanted to capture. They weren't seedy. It didn't feel dodgy. Believe me, I wouldn't have sat there with my boobs out if it had.'

Lottie and Beth are giggling like monkeys, but I look sidewards at Matt who's staring into the fire. I take it he's aware that while the distraction is a good thing, I'm not really up for having too much of a laugh right now. Dad's on the missing list and it's off-key. We wait for the story to finish.

'Of course, what started as a cliché, ended as one,' sighs Michaela. 'David and I decided we'd seen all we could stomach and had got all the talking head shots we could use. So we went outside and got dressed.

Then they all flipped out ... and I picked up the camera again.'

The three men and two girls ran out into the open, still naked. Jenny threw herself on the ground, boobs wobbling, and the three guys racked out three lines of coke, like a bikini in a triangle, around her crotch. 'I guess the condensation would have made the drugs soggy inside?' says Michaela to me. Why me? I'm convinced I must look like a trampy blonde cokehead to everyone. I guess so, I reply.

'They took it in turns to snort a line and the last one gave her a little tickle down there too. The other guys were jolting around, about to explode. I turned the camera to the other girl, Chloë, who's standing, naked, on her own, looking down expectantly at the ground, blatantly wondering if she was in for seconds.'

Everyone expels a sigh of camped-up revulsion.

'Anyway, that was more than enough for me. It's not like we can use any of it ... The point is everyone's here for something different. Whether they know it when they arrive or not.'

Michaela looks at me. The flames reflect in her eyes and I'm envious of her drive to present truths whatever their shape or form. 'What's your take on it? You must have seen it all.'

Now she has me. Where do I start? I'm panicked: the intellectual spin on her everyday vocabulary gets me fishing around for anything I can remember from a poorly attended term's worth of social anthropology at uni.

'Well, at one end of the continuum,' I say, 'you've got the ones who arrive with a carefully plotted out schedule of every single band they want to see and they stick to it. They'll be banging on about the best bits in chat rooms and around pub tables until next summer. Equally as predictable, but right at the other end, are the nutters with the single goal of being off their faces for seventy-two hours. Somewhere in the middle are the majority of us who have a vague idea of what we'd like to do – bands we might check out, mates we're on the lookout for. Inevitably we end up spannered, doing little of what we'd imagined, but that's when the magic happens. That's why people come back year in, year out.

'It's the leap into the unknown, giving in to something beyond your control,' I continue, surprised at myself for having relatively intelligent thoughts at this time of night for once. 'You can't set out to have prescribed crazy experiences, can you? All those bloody adverts for phone companies set at festivals, desperately trying to be cool, insipidly and predictably suggesting what might happen if you're with their network, are utter crap. All that sort of imagery does is encourage us to miss the point. Forget your bloody phone signal. It's all about the ley lines converging, isn't it?'

'In my opinion,' I explain, 'subconsciously, a lot of the people are here for change on some level. That it's all become some sort of an endurance test, a rite of passage.'

I look over at Matt, who's concentrating hard, thinking about what I'm saying, and I pull a face, sheepishly.

'I'm really interested in the whole journey idea too,' says Michaela. The woman never stops working, she might as well have the camera on me, and she goes in for the kill with her soft BBC-standard-therapy-speak: 'What about you? What do you want out of it? You're not immune just because you make a living from observing others for a few hours.'

I bring my dirty knees up under my chin. Think about the question, then hope Michaela fills the silence with another one so I can dodge it. She doesn't. She's incredibly good at her job. I feel professionally obliged to give her an honest answer to the question she's chucked at me and feel utterly amazed when I hear my own voice.

'I came down here hoping to bust out of a stalemate I'd got into with my husband actually.'

I can literally hear Beth and Lottie's ears prick up. Matt creates some very obvious space between us and I look into the flames, still carried along by the same wave of resignation and recognition that had swept the first sentence out of my mouth.

'Thing is, what I didn't realise is that we started off at a crossroads ... He's off getting completely nutted and doesn't look like he ever wants to come back down to earth. Whereas I can't wait for the morning.'

I'm shocked that I've just opened my heart in front of a load of strangers. The others don't say a word. I turn to Matt. He looks pretty shocked too.

'I'm done ... I need to lie down. I can't stay upright any longer.' I don't ask him if he wants to stay, just say 'Come on' and pull him to his feet. He puts his arm around me, says goodnight to everyone and we walk off.

Twenty-five

'He's back, love. Dad's back.' It's my mum.

I had spent hours lying down desperately willing the phone to ring and my heart had felt like it'd relocated to my throat permanently. Once my body finally caved in and I'd drifted off, it rang.

My mum's girly voice has become stronger and more singular recently. She's slight with delicate features, looks far younger than she is, and more or less lives in ballet pumps, neat boot-cut jeans and modest stretchy cotton tops. I imagine her sitting on the arm of their cream leather sofa in her M&S grey jersey pyjamas.

It's five thirty and daylight is already poking its way inside at the tent's entrance. Along one side the magenta fabric has become pinky orange with the sunrise. My eyes sting from lack of sleep, my skin feels like it doesn't belong to me and my windpipe feels so narrow I can only push out a whisper. 'How is he?'

'Exhausted but in one piece. The police found him wandering around the town about three-quarters of an hour ago.'

I can't say anything else as I slowly become conscious. The back of my head sinks down further into the pillows as the tension that had turned my shoulders to rock outside the karaoke tent immediately begins to disperse.

'I'm just about to put him in the bath before the doctor gets here.'

Exactly what everyone had suspected had indeed happened. Dad had gone out, lost track of time and place, then started to flag with the heat. On the outside, he and the dog were suffering with little more than blisters, sore paws, sunburn and the disorientating effects of a hot day in the sun without anything to eat or drink. Inside, though, what he'd been through was almost too heartbreaking to think about.

Dad sobbed and sobbed when he stepped back into my mum's arms. She eventually managed to decipher that throughout the day not one person he'd asked for water had helped him. A frightened, helpless man and not one bastard helped him. Each refusal was a small, cruel act that had hit him hard.

When he gets confused, my dad stutters and slurs, never finishes a sentence. In his old dog-walking jeans and trainers, he must have seemed like the village idiot and those small-minded drones turned away, ignored him, leaving him thirsty and even more distressed.

It's fantastic that he's back in the safety of my parents' magnolia-and-beige house, with its brass picture frames, marble fireplace and conservatory extension, but the terrible truth of what is looming ahead of him seeps into my mind. Last night was a watershed, an indicator of the creeping darkness into which he'll be swallowed.

'I'm coming home.' I'm wide awake. I want to help.

'You don't have to do that, Louisa. Pop in next weekend. We're fine . . . I'm sorry I had to worry you, I just didn't want you to hear something and panic.' Silence. She tries to reassure me that everything's back to normal. All I can think of, though, is the pair of them, trapped. In their brand-new house with its badly built walls already showing weakness with the strain of the rosewood curtain rails and linen–cotton mix cream curtains my mum has at every window.

'Anyway, how's Dan? I hope all this hasn't ruined your weekend.'

I can't lie. 'He's not here, Mum. We both hung out with different friends last night. You know what he's like.'

She makes a very obvious job of not wanting to pry and we hang up.

In other circumstances she would have picked up on the loud, guttural snoring coming from the throat of the man lying next to me. A few hours earlier Matt and I had sat on either edge of the bed, both of us yawning, making a meal out of how tired we were, hammily signalling to one another that sleep was definitely the only thing on the agenda. There was awkwardness at the strangeness of the evening that had unfolded. We were alone and about to share a mattress; fully clothed, we gingerly committed to it horizontally.

Eventually, half asleep, he put his arm around me. I lay curled up, staring at the weave in the rattan flooring, and soon began to hear snorty rumblings that rapidly rose in volume as Matt slipped into a deep sleep.

Now, in the pinky, orange tones of the tent, I watch his tummy rising and falling with each noisy vibration, stressing the buttons on the black shirt, which is finally crumpled. The waistband of his white cotton boxers is slightly higher than that of his low-slung shorts and an inch or so of milky flesh above that, covered in spidery pubic hair, is exposed. He's not my type but I can't deny I'm incredibly attracted to him.

Eyes still stinging but head full with the contents of the brief conversation I've just had with my mum, I am gently surprised at the ease with which I am intimately studying the private moments of the sleeping man on the bed. I reach for my sunglasses, get up and head outside.

Twenty-six

Almost anyone who's up this early, besides me, probably hasn't been to bed. Odds on they'll be over at Wild Wood where a red-and-white big top is tucked in a clearing behind the Meadows. The only way to get to it is via a small footbridge and a little trek through the trees.

The early-morning mist is lifting and although Wild Wood isn't the magical Tim Burton-directed other-world I remember, seeing it through sober eyes, it remains fantastically surreal.

A woman with wavy blonde hair, head to toe in green-and-gold body paint, is posing astride an enormous white horse. I can see cracks in the paint that follow the lines around her eyes and the wrinkles on her forehead. She's not doing much apart from getting off on the fact that she looks like an extra in a trippy medieval fairy tale. Anyway, she probably fancies herself as Stevie Nicks in the good old days, but she's more like Bonnie Tyler in an episode of *Doctor Who*. Two kids in knitted hoodies, both under ten, kick around barefoot on the grass behind her. They look bored. Fed up of waiting for their mum's drugs to wear off.

A small unruly column of four neatly moustached First World War soldiers march through the hundreds of bodies and empty plastic cups littering the grass outside the big top. Two rangy geezers with high-lighted mullets in baggy jeans, T-shirts, trainers and ball gowns over the top try to fall in too. In the middle of all this, a lone traveller guy with a ponytail and a goatee is standing and dancing like he's in an old Prodigy video. He's ducking and dodging around to an old acid-house track that's playing in his head. I can't resist a smile.

Bart, Helena and Nelson are ruined. Leaning back on their elbows among the debris, looking into the early-morning sun from behind the cheap kids' novelty sunglasses they picked up God knows where. I knew they'd be here, still gurning, chewing the insides of their cheeks, so I called Bart on the way over to find out where exactly.

Even though the weekend has been a write-off in so many ways, something massive, something good happened last night. I finally saw my life for what it is: a shoddy, selfish and demeaning exercise in going out, coming down, fucking up and getting by. Last night I finally pulled my head out of my arse for long enough to remember that this is not what I'd had in mind for myself when I left school.

Bart can hardly say a word without trailing off into nowhere but is convinced I disappeared into the night to shag Matt and keeps looking out from behind his pink Mr Chatterbox frames at me and grinning. He can think what he likes right now. Helena and Nelson both tap the fingers on their right hands to the beat of the old ska tune coming out of the big top.

I sit cross-legged, staring with them into the sun, listening to them talking in semicircles, repeatedly going up and down the conversational equivalent of well-trodden cul-de-sacs. It's enough at the moment just to be listening, to be close to my friends' voices as they stop and start, and watching as another two men and a girl with painted faces, sequinned shorts and DMs make the seemingly huge decision whether or not to sit down a few feet away.

Bart's droopy skin is greasy and thick dark shiny stubble pokes through. I rub my fingers over his cheek and he dopily swats me away. I've started to take on board some of his frustrations with me, but this isn't the right time to talk about it. I think it through again instead and squirm at how much patience he's had with me.

I pull a biro out of the small bag I'm wearing across Lottie's sweatshirt and write a note on Bart's forearm. *Twatface. You're a goon. You MUST call me when you're back home. Louisa xxx.* He'll never remember if I tell him now that we need to talk but I certainly don't want any excuse to duck out of the long overdue humble-pie conversation that I owe him.

He can't read the upside-down scribble and calls me a knobhead. I write the message again the other way up on the inside of his pale, skinny arm so that he can. 'You're still a knobhead,' he says. I can smell that he's farted too and he's smiling, pleased with his fragrant gift to me. I try to smile back without breathing.

I'm glad I don't feel completely out of tune with them. I can appreciate the perverted beauty of the decadent, grubby carnival of avoidance that's pulsating around us. My mind is spinning off on tangents and spiralling inwards and back out again from lack of sleep and days of boozing. Like them, I'm greedily eating up the sunrise with every shallow, stinky breath I take.

Unlike them my heightened awareness comes from a very different place. In the last seventy-two hours I've had my nose rubbed in reality; over the course of the

weekend, there have been two separate police investi-
gations into the disappearances of, arguably, the two
most important men in my life.

So it's more than fine by me that nothing, in real
terms, is happening here. Just a big bunch of people
talking twaddle to anyone who'll listen while the rest
pace around, in and out of view. A perfect purgatory
before the day starts for real.

Bart starts twitching, sniffs the air and puts his
mouth to my ear. 'I've got terrible wind.'

'You don't say.' I bump on my bum away from him,
hold my nose.

'I'm going to have to have a walk around.' He gets
up and reaches down to me. 'Come on. If anyone says
anything I'm going to blame you.'

'Fuck you, Fart Coleman.' I get up and follow him
into the big top anyway.

Inside a white parrot swoops down in front of us
and lands on the shoulder of a tall, dark-haired man
with black, thick-framed, square glasses. The parrot sits
obediently, head tilted, beak ajar as his master talks at
him through tight lips. In a well-tailored black suit jacket
over a white cotton vest and smart black sweatpants,
he's clutching a cane with a silver-and-black art deco
handle in a fist cluttered with oversized silver Gothic
rings.

'That's what the devil would look like if he worked

at one of the blokes' fashion mags,' I whisper. The man turns his head in our direction and smiles.

We go further into the warm mist of the dawn freak show, through a cast of rinsed-out cabaret performers, club kids, Special Brew wasters and thirty-something middle-management men. Bart points to the bald-headed bloke spinning Lee Scratch Perry from the velvet-draped DJ booth wearing a giant blue-and-red Tesco loyalty card as a sandwich board over his naked torso. It's Gavin Jerk, one of a line of performance artists who use a stage name that's a bastardised version of someone else's. He was big on the alternative scene at the same time as Gavin Turk, Tracey Emin, Damien Hirst and all the other YBAs who made it big in the nineties. This is where he'd disappeared to.

My legs have had it. I prop myself up against the edge of the boxing ring in the middle of the big top and light a cigarette. Inside, on a floor lined with animal skins, is a tiny contortionist. Her white costume and overall look mimics a prepubescent Soviet gymnast from the seventies, bar the cut-out rectangular panel across her chest that puts her porcelain double AAs on view. Her jet-black hair is plaited into a crown on top of her head and two plain white round plastic plasters cover her nipples. She's flanked by two square-jawed men wearing white all-in-one gym suits and feathered bowler hats.

We both stand mesmerised at the positions she pulls herself into and the elegance with which she then begins to juggle three delicate egg shapes.

The last time I'd seen a contortionist was at a dreadful party to celebrate the launch of a crappy new alcopop. The Soho bar was decked out more like a chintzy Essex bordello rather than the speakeasy the organisers were going for. I'd arrived early, six thirtyish on a Monday or Tuesday night, and had arranged to meet Dan there so we could soak up as many free drinks as possible before heading off somewhere else.

He'd turned up with Alistair, already half cut from an afternoon boozing in the City, armed with some knock-off Agent Provocateur knickers he'd bought for me from a bloke in the pub. Unfortunately for the girl twisting into shapes that night, some bright spark from the drinks company decided it would be a bit risqué if she rest a bowl of lightly salted Nachos on her pubic bone and create a little table with her body. Dan and Alistair hilariously suggested that people dip into the Snatchos, over and over again. I yanked both of them into the lobby, balled them out and stormed off home.

Bart's absolutely hypnotised by the bastard offspring of Olga Korbut. I prod him gently. 'Maybe you should invite her back to your tent for a game of Twister.'

His nose resting on his elbows, he nods, mentally

flaccid and unable to bite back with any banter. 'I could watch her all day,' is all he manages.

Unfortunately, Bart's arse is as relaxed as everything else in his body and he lets off another corker. I leave him enthralled by Olga junior.

I could go on like this forever. The party never stops and it's always a similar – if not the same – bunch of weird people lurking around. I head back outside with the sense that if I come back here in five years' time, probably to the hour, nothing much will have changed.

'Louisa . . . How you doing?'

Springing up from the grass, where he had been sat with a couple of cute rockabilly girls, Paul Vincent bounces across my path. He's smiling but wobbles around so much that he has to lean into me. I help him steady himself for a moment or two until he steps back into his own space. He has scummy white bits in between his teeth and is wearing his laminated press pass like a medal. 'What's happening?' he asks, clearly oblivious to the state I'd left his web report in. This is awful. I try not to sound jaded in the face of the enthusiasm that he is still able to muster, at this time of the morning, but I don't want to get too matey either. He's just one in a long stream of fresh-out-of-college kids who drop into our office every now and then, armed with ideas and eager to work for nothing if it means getting their name in print. Still, what I'd done to the website was pathetic – I'd been just the same, equally as eager, at his age – and I don't want to be two-faced now to boot.

I pass him my water bottle and he takes a swig.

'Just kicking around, Paul. You know.'

'What a weekend. It's really set the bar for the rest of the summer. Everyone's saying it's been the best year for ages.'

'Really?' Not from where I've been standing, but then, apart from the orchestra in the jazz tent, I hadn't even got round to catching a band play. 'I don't think I've got into the swing of things properly this year,' I say diplomatically.

He offers me a fag even though I'm still smoking one Bart gave me. 'No shit. Well, still time, I guess.'

Incredibly, at this time of the morning, he then starts asking me if I think Alexa's planning on getting him to do more for the magazine, and perhaps we could go for a coffee soon, to talk about some feature ideas.

Yeah, right. Whatever. If he's not already realised that he's far more capable of doing my job than I am, he will do soon.

Younger. Cheaper. Still seduced by it all and still able to shrug off a king-size hangover by 10 a.m. to start work. Even more importantly, when he does have the opportunity to put pen to paper, for more than a caption story, he makes a bloody good job of it.

What is it about that poxy magazine, though? What is it that brings out so much of the worst in people? The levels of desperation to be part of it, to get on the inside, are astonishing. I wonder if I should tell Paul, for instance, about a stylist that used to work a lot with us. Never got paid, always worked her butt off for the tear sheets, spurred on by the hope that she'd get a job on the fashion team, or a lucrative advertising campaign off the back of it. It never happened and she wound up getting pinched by store detectives for stealing hundred quid a pop photography books in Selfridges just before Christmas.

Really want to do this? I want to say. Do this properly? Go and get a job on a local paper in the sticks and learn your craft.

Fuck it. What's the point? Look at how pleased he is with his press pass. Instead, I tell him to call me when we're back in London, that my mates are waiting for me.

I find Helena and Nelson sitting quietly, spacing out, until the music switches. Gavin Jerk, the DJ, must be on the early-morning irony tip as 'Pacific State' by 808 State filters out to us. Everyone gasps as a couple of blokes in football tops lob small camping gas canisters into the woods. They explode and wild screams and yelps of approval fill the air. A foam mushroom and an onion jump up and start dancing to the old rave track.

That's it. I'm exhausted. I need my bed. I'm not staying a moment more. I bend down, plant huge kisses on Helena and Nelson's foreheads and leave.

Twenty-seven

I stop off to pick up a carton of orange juice. My internal battery icon is flashing empty, faintly and pathetically. I survey the temporary shop that operates as a round-the-clock general store and crisis relief zone. It has everything from plasters and pear cider to wellies and dog food. There's a banner above the till listing an amalgamation of big global humanitarian charities that its profits benefit.

The queue is at least ten deep. The guy on the till has red, sore, tired eyes and a couple of empty cans of Red Bull are lined up on the ledge behind him. Three young kids try to scrape together the money to pay for a new tent. A ragtag bag of misadventurists wobble around the store. One guy is reading war poetry to another. There are wonderfully ruined fools everywhere, picking up tins, earnestly studying ingredients lists, yawning, pulling up hoods and stretching sleeves over their hands.

A girl in an orange furry hat, with eyes on the front and a big snout instead of a peak, bangs her basket into the back of my knees. I turn and look down at some jumbo Tampax and a packet of Nurofen. I stare at the girl's dirty feet and then down at my own.

The shabby precursor to this whole sorry trip, the episode after work on Thursday, eventually wins the space in my head it has been fighting for. While the guy on the till rings through lighters, toilet rolls, bags of Haribo and some Ecover laundry liquid, I hold a hand over my wrinkled brow and it plays out in full, frame by frame, in sharp widescreen detail.

I'd popped out of the office early afternoon to discover that summer had finally kicked off and the sun had burnt through the fresh damp air I'd journeyed to work in. People sat on kerbs outside pubs wearing flip-flops, drinking pints and the front page of the *Evening Standard* announced the beginning of a heatwave. Nailbars were full of girls getting emergency pedicures. I ditched grabbing a sandwich at Pret and made a beeline for Topshop at Oxford Circus to look for some new shorts.

On the way I called Dan. He was in a pub, somewhere in the City, with Tom. I reminded him we had an early start in the morning. Half an hour later, I called back to ask whether he'd like me to pick him up some new shorts too – H&M is just across the road – and his phone was switched off.

It's impossible to stay sitting at your desk in Soho when the sun has decided to make its first serious appearance of the year. By the time I got back to the office, there had been an exodus to the pub a few doors down. Even Alexa was fixing her make-up, preparing to meet her boyfriend who was on the roof at Soho House.

I hadn't managed to find any shorts in Topshop. I improvised with some big turn-ups on my jeans but the heat of the sun beating down against the denim was too much. I kept my legs tucked under a wooden trestle pub table and joined Cherry, our receptionist, *Neon*'s music ed Jason and his girlfriend Stacey in drinking vodka cranberry like it's Ribena. As the throng around the pub swelled, I got up, slouched around and clinked glasses with the world and his wife.

Minutes melted away, hours floated by, people came and people went. I chatted with the skinny shop boys from the boutique a couple of doors down from us, three sisters who run a festival of short films, a guy who used to be in *Coronation Street*, half the staff of a massive ad agency and even Jason's mum, who'd stopped by after a visit to the National Gallery.

It was dusky when Andrew Glass, our ad manager,

showed up, on his way back to the office after some client drinks. He's been at the mag since spring but I hadn't had much to do with him. He's the spit of a housemate's boyfriend from uni. She dumped him after a couple of weeks because his willy was so wide. Nothing to do with length, just width. Sex was painful and, frankly, grotesque. The guy's dimensions quickly became legendary in Social Sciences and his disproportion earned him a nickname, the Stump, all over campus.

It was only on Thursday night that I managed to swerve the mental obstacle this likeness had thrown in the way of talking to Andrew much beyond anything our jobs required. Stupidly, though, I told Cherry quietly about Andrew's resemblance to the Stump and she of course shared it with him immediately afterwards.

Andrew was noble in the face of this affront to his genitals and rather than respond with cheap macho retorts, he inadvertently made me feel bad about the miserly welcome I had given him in the office. He shrugged it off, changed the subject and said how much he'd enjoyed a reportage piece I'd written about professional Bond Street shoplifters for our last issue.

Cherry took off for the loo and was gone for ages. We passed the time and somehow, from nowhere, in the way it just does, a funny little bit of something started building between us. He looked at me for a bit too long when he spoke and I asked if I could have a closer look at the detail on his watch face. When a glass collector pushed past us to get back through the scrum on the street, we leant into each other for fractionally longer than was necessary. It was not especially sophisticated or imaginative but it was enough.

'Shit. Shit. Shit.' Andrew started kicking the kerb. 'It's my sister's birthday tomorrow and I've forgotten to buy her present. Bollocks.'

'No worries,' I said, holding his forearm. 'I've got piles of stuff that's been sent in to me.' It was all sitting on my desk, not even opened. I said I'd put a little package together for him.

I didn't bother to switch on any of the office lights. There was a dull amber glow coming in from the street, just enough to make out what I was doing. I clattered around my desk, made dents in posh-looking cardboard bags and upended Jiffy bags packed with CDs and press releases.

I shoved a Diptyque candle, some Chanel nail polish and a pink-and-white polka-dot memory stick into Andrew's hands then headed into the meeting room. I poked about looking for the crate of booze I'd seen in there. Andrew followed me and when I turned back to head out with a bottle of gin, I bumped into him and stayed too close for a little too long.

It was the clumsy beginnings of a predictable, urgent and inelegant fumble, brought on by little more than all-day drinking, a bit of lame flirting and the intimacy of the darkness. Perhaps, in retrospect, it might not feel so bad had there been something more to it.

He pushed me onto the table and I shunted a plate of half-eaten sandwiches, left from a meeting earlier in the afternoon, away from my head. My heart raced almost as quickly as the whole thing unfolded. I put my hand inside his T-shirt at the same time kicking my pants off from where they were hanging on my ankles. I felt what I imagined to be milky white skin. My knickers remained stuck around my right ankle.

Despite the thickness of the balmy evening air, the flesh I touched was cold, echoing how foreign it was to me. The ripe smell of overheated egg mayo wafted around. An underlying current slowly began to sweep across my brain, suggesting that it was all wrong.

While Andrew jolted around in the shadows in front of me, pulling his jeans and pants off, hopping in the race to get them down, I became certain that there was no way I could have sex with this man. It would be an absolute and despicable act of betrayal against my husband. I was not that woman. Dan might switch his phone off and stay out all night drinking with his mates but that didn't warrant me lying on a table in a dark room where another man's naked erect penis was a few inches away from my crotch.

I grabbed my pants, buried them in my handbag and

ran off out of the office, into the street. All I wanted to do was get home. Why the fuck hadn't I just done that after work like I'd planned to? I was racked with guilt, shocked at what I'd let happen. Gutted at how I was full to the brim of good intentions that never come good.

I am saved from beating myself up for too long with Thursday's sordid memory, by the beginning of 'Thriller' by Michael Jackson. At the shop's entrance four zombies with white faces, fake blood and black teeth stoop, sway and kick out a little dance routine like the one in the video. Another zombie mans a portable CD player with mini speakers.

The guy on the till yawns. The zombies have been here five or six times already since yesterday evening. 'It was funny just before midnight,' he says to me as he rings through my carton of juice.

Twenty-eight

I'm sitting in a low, pink vinyl-covered armchair, head down, reading out loud from the book on my lap. The peach hospital walls have seen better days. Speckled with chips and dents exposing chalky white plaster. Grubby with splashes of brown gloop that came courtesy of a metal meal trolley weeks back.

Halfway through the first page I notice thick lines of dirt under each of my thumbnails and reach for the carton of blue, anti-infection jelly in a white plastic wire holder that is attached to the bedside cabinet. As I rub the alcohol gel into my hands, slowly, I stare at the young man in the bed.

David Lester's face is purple and swollen. The lids of his eyes, bulbous and shiny. The oxygen mask covering his mouth has a yellow tinge to it and he is surrounded by an armoury of beeping and dripping machinery. I'd told the nurses I was a friend and they let me straight in. I couldn't give a shit if the police find out I've been here.

I start reading again. It's a short story. An essay by Tom Wolfe written in the sixties, called 'The Noonday Underground'. Sam, my boyfriend at uni, had told me I should read it halfway through the first term. I did and it got under my skin. Sam and I are still good friends.

Now, it's a pleasure to share with someone else the romance of Larry Lynch, a sharp-suited, working-class kid from Brixton. How he slips away from his desk in the West End at lunchtimes to dance like a maniac and get his midweek fix of 'The Mod Life' for an hour in a basement club somewhere off Oxford Street.

A nurse comes in the door behind me and checks the valve on David's drip, writes on the notes on the clipboard at the end of his bed and interrupts to ask if I want a cup of tea. I nod and carry on reading. Milk? Sugar? I nod for milk and then shake my head for sugar. I don't want to spoil the prose any more than I have already with my poor American inflections. You'd think a nurse would have more sensitivity.

I plough on, determined to entertain the heavily bandaged guy lying in mint-green and white sheets next to me. I watch his eyes for any movement whenever I pause to emphasise the end of a paragraph. He's still asleep but I feel I'm connecting, that Tom Wolfe's words are penetrating his battered skull.

Light, soft-soled footsteps come back into the room and a voice muffles away behind me. I start to get irritated by that fucking nurse, her fucking tea and her fucking chit-chat, but know I need to keep calm, for David. I feel a hand on my right shoulder and gently try to shrug it off. I want to finish the story without any interruptions. It can only be ten pages long.

'I thought I'd find you here.'

I shrug the hand away again but it starts to shake my shoulder much harder now.

'Louisa. Stop talking. Wake up.'

I slowly come to and the blurred shape bent over me sharpens into focus. It's Alexa.

'Late night, was it?'

I'm still confused, still half asleep. What time is it? I ask.

'Oh, round about two. Round about the time yesterday I had to eat shit at your no-show, grovel to the head of press at EMI and do your fucking interview myself, Louisa. All while I should have been kissing arse with the director of entertainment for Channel 4, who wants to give *Neon* its own show.'

I look around my tent. No sign of Matt. What time did he go? He was still snoring his head off when I'd crept back in this morning. It's boiling hot. My lips are stuck together but my armpits are damp. Alexa throws a bottle of water down onto the bed.

'Come on. Get it together. You and I need to have a serious conversation.'

A wasp buzzes around me. I bat it away and splash my face with the Evian. The wasp keeps coming back for more. Alexa's sharp auburn bob looks more severe than normal against the flimsy cotton shift dress and cream kung fu shoes she has on.

She sits down on the pink leather sofa just across from the bed, milky, freckly limbs crossed.

I refresh my ponytail into a new knot at the back of my head with my fingers, drag my legs around and sit upright on the edge of the bed just a few feet across from her.

'Hold on.' I pull the tent flap open above the bed and the sunlight shines right on top of me. 'I'm sorry,' I begin, shuffling along out of the square of light.

Alexa wrinkles her nose. 'It's disgusting in here, Louisa. Let's get this over with, shall we? Quickly?'

I ask her if it would be better if we went over to the coffee bar – I could do with a hit of caffeine before she massacres me – but she snaps back: 'If you think I'm about to air my dirty laundry outside, in front of half the magazine's bloody advertisers . . . no fucking way. You can talk to me here.'

I stare down at my dust-covered feet and shins and

then back up again, conscious that I've presented my boss with greasy stripes of bleached hair criss-crossing on the crown of my head. My sloppiness is endemic. I shake my head slowly from side to side, look straight at her. 'Things have got to change. I know I've let you down.'

She raises her fine ginger eyebrows, impressed that, for once, I was over doling out cock-and-bull excuses. Alexa stands up and paces over to the far end of the tent. 'You're damn right, Louisa. Things are changing ...' She picks up the *Rough Guide to the Kama Sutra* and drops it down again on the coffee table. 'What on earth happened to you? I thought you had real potential. You weren't the most obvious choice for the job – ' she gives my sweatshirt-over-black-foil-dress ensemble the once-over – 'but I thought you could pull it off.' Alexa's commiserating with me for not being one of her clones and at the same time congratulating herself for having the balls to let me loose in the pages of her beloved magazine. I can live with that. She loves the sound of her own voice. I let her carry on with her speech. The quicker she gets it over with, the sooner I can get my sorry arse back to London.

Her blue eyes with their light orange lashes lock straight into mine and only then do I suss what's coming. This is no regular bollocking. 'You just don't seem to want it though, and even if you did, after this weekend you've left me with no choice . . . I'm letting you go, Louisa.'

She looks down at the floor; her angular posture slips into something slightly more human as she waits for me to say something. To beg for one more chance probably.

Matt had left his number scribbled down on a compliments slip from his B & B. I lean over and pick it up, still taking in the last couple of sentences. A wave of nausea brings with it the surreal feeling that getting the boot might not be such a bad thing.

Infuriated at my lack of fight, she morphs back into Alexa the Hun. 'Are you listening to me, Louisa? I'm firing you.'

Even with the Evian my lips remain stuck together. I purse them even closer, hang my head down trying to work out what to say. What seemed glamorous and fun has become a drag. The parties and perks that are the pay-off for the terrible wages I earn have become dull and predictable. I'm sick to the back teeth of sorting through my party invites by working out which events will have the best canapés (I can never afford decent food of my own) and which one's goody bags are likely to contain the highest value presents or vouchers. In fact, if it means I'm spared the indignity of lunging for even one more goody bag at the end of the night, Alexa can stick her job.

There's nothing I'm prepared to share that can further this conversation in any meaningful way. The silence has thrown her. Alexa came here anticipating a shouting match and is surprised to find herself saying everything she had planned to in much calmer tones than she'd expected. I feel like telling her that this way is much better for the both of us, but don't.

'Like I said, Louisa, you've left me with no option. The traffic on Friday was just one of those things, and the police turning up in the media centre, in front of everyone, to ask me questions about your husband beating the living daylights out of some poor kid isn't technically your fault either.' She pulls at the gold Chanel logo pendant that hangs on a waist-length chain down from her tiny neck. 'Although we were going to have to have serious words about that back in the office.'

My head aches with caffeine cravings and the sick feeling at the back of my throat melds with it. Goddammit Alexa, get it over with. Tell me you know it was me, that I was the imbecile who wrote a whole load of rude words on the *Neon* website.

'Even the interview yesterday could have been glossed over.' She ruffles her hands through her hair, preening. 'The readers do find interviews by the editor a bit more of an event, so despite all the chaos you caused it will have actually worked out for the better in the magazine.

No, it's the stunt you pulled on Friday night that I can't brush off. Let's not beat around the bush – we both know it was you that wrecked Paul's online report, don't we?'

I hold my hands up in admission and finally squeeze some words out. I think she's been fair, I tell her. I'll be in sometime during the week to clear my desk.

Twenty-nine

The steam drifting upwards from the red-hot black coffee mists up my sunglasses. Bart always calls me asbestos head: with the same ease that my scalp tolerates the most potent peroxide permitted under health and safety laws, without the slightest bit of tingling, the inside of my mouth and throat just love scalding liquids. A notch below boiling is how I like my tea and coffee. Lukewarm and they're down the sink.

I prod the bacon roll in front of me and scrape the onions out. I'm not hungry but the drive home will take at least four hours, especially with all the Sunday early-evening traffic heading back into London, and I don't want to have to pull over the minute I hit the motorway. The first scratchy dry bite goes down uncomfortably.

The conversation with Alexa is beginning to settle.

An hour ago I was Louisa Parker, Features Editor of *Neon*. Now, I'm plain Louisa Parker.

Sitting on a wooden stool, fiddling with my car keys and picking at the bacon roll, I watch everyone milling around the Boutique Field. Mostly they're weathered and relaxed. Some have got the Sunday papers tucked under their arms. Lottie walks straight past with her kids and the nanny but doesn't spot me. I think better of shouting a hello. Her sweatshirt is back in my tent and returning it is the perfect excuse to call Matt with later in the week. I'll have time to wash it too.

I stir my coffee, aimlessly, and carry on thinking about Alexa. She's mad as a hatter but absolutely dedicated to that magazine. I, quite clearly, was not. The swanky lifestyle – all the parties, gifts and press trips – is fantastic and there's no way I'm going to start seriously complaining about it, but it has come to eclipse what really excited me about working at *Neon* in the first place. I had set out to use the job as the industry-standard stepping stone; I saw it as a terribly paid but hugely credible position leading to something more serious, better paid and, ultimately, even more credible. Instead I'd got greedy with the perks, stayed too long and completely forgotten that becoming a better writer was why I was there in the first place.

I can't blame Alexa for giving me the boot. I'd fire

me. Matt was right. It is time to get a grown-up job.

'The Noonday Underground', the story I was reading in my dream, is all about a bunch of kids who are part of 'The Scene'. All that matters to them is being in the right club, with the right hair, the right clothes, dancing to the right music among the right people, at the right time.

Which is OK if you're a fifteen-year-old mod living in London in the sixties. But I'm over thirty.

A little while back my brother had tried to convince me that I didn't have to be at the centre of the in-crowd to be happy. I had shown up, for the umpteenth time, at my parents', exhausted, emotional and crying at virtually anything after a couple of weeks of heavy partying and missing deadlines.

My older brother had been drafted in by Mum to get to the bottom of what was wrong with me this time. We went to the local Harvester. I ordered a double Scotch to take the edge off my comedown and mask the smell of fried scampi and chips.

He told me that, although I might think my life looked great, it seemed far from it. Then he – a regular guy, married with a couple of kids, living in the same backwater we grew up in – mentioned the unmention-able. 'I suppose you've been taking drugs . . .' I looked down at the floor like an embarrassed adolescent, thinking, what the bloody hell does he know about it?

He's probably got it into his head that I'm injecting smack or something stupid.

Anyway, now the bigger sentiment behind what he was trying to say is beginning to make much more sense. One look at the state of me and a few beers down the Harvester on a Friday night can't seem like such a bad place to be.

I'm not about to up sticks and head for them but I do pick up the phone to call my brother. To say hi and let him know I'll be around in the next few days. It's time to turn things on their head, start looking after my parents. It's shameful the way I've been carrying on; not so much as a phone call all week and then turning up expecting to be babysat through my comedowns.

Fucking thing. The phone's finally dead. Of all the times to run out of battery. I pull my shades off and rub my eyes. It'll have to wait until tomorrow. Still, maybe the phone dying isn't such a bad thing; under normal circumstances I can't bear to be out of the loop but if ever there were a case for an enforced time out, this is it.

Unfortunately it isn't going to happen just yet. I hear someone shout my name and take my hand away from my face. It's Amita. She's striding towards me, in fresh Sunday gear too: denim mini, tight gingham short-sleeved shirt and flip-flops.

'What's up?' I ask. She looks serious. The guy she

was with yesterday's nowhere to be seen. I bet they've had a ruck. Amita always comes running when she's got man trouble. I want to be there for her but I can't deal with anyone else's problems right now, especially hers. 'You're lucky you caught me, I'm just about to pack my stuff and leave.'

She shakes her head. 'What's with your phone? I've been trying to call you. You can't leave. Not yet. Dan's back.'

'And?' If she thinks I'm wasting another minute on that lame excuse for a man, she's mistaken. Dan's in serious trouble. It's out of my hands and I can't control what's going to happen to him, or us, now. It's gone past that. He can make his own way back to London, and by the time he gets home, I'll be back on the road, down to my parents' place.

I need some time with them. I want to let them know I'm going to be around a lot more. Plus, I need time out before I tackle Dan, to digest what's happened this weekend, the whole kit and kaboodle, so when I speak to him next I'll have worked out what it all means for me.

'If he's stupid enough to come back here in full daylight, the police are welcome to him. I'm not wiping his arse for him any more.'

'Fair enough,' she answers, blinking slowly and raising her eyebrows as if to say keep your hair on. 'He's completely off his head. I thought you'd want to get him cleaned up before he gets pulled in. That was all. Anyway, what happened to you last night?'

'What? Nothing.' I'll tell her about Dad when I'm up for answering all the questions.

'One minute you're outside having a fag with Matt. The next minute the pair of you've fucked off. Really? Nothing happened?'

'Nothing happened,' I say firmly.

'Could have fooled me. I bumped into him on the way over here, I was totally stressing out, you know, with the Dan drama, and the second I mention that I was about to help you sort out your dipshit of a husband, he stopped in his tracks and turned back.'

It's the icing on the cake. What must he be making of that? What on earth must he be thinking of me now? I want to throttle Amita but she's only trying to do me a favour. I mustn't take any of this out on her.

'Look, thanks, Am, I've had a lot going on,' I say, pulling her into me for a hug. 'Let's get this over and done with. There's no way I'm driving Dan all the way back home though. One of those other idiots can do it.'

Thirty

'Louisa. There.' Am's huge bumpy nose is pointing in the direction of a clapped-out bicycle with both wheels fixed to a frame on the floor, preventing it from going anywhere.

Immediately I recognise the sinewy hunched-up body sat on it, pedalling nineteen to the dozen, as my husband's.

The bike is poking out of the front of an awning under which half a dozen sweaty, shirtless, tattoo-heavy crusties are hopping around from one foot to another in baggy parachute trousers and camo shorts, like they're dancing on hot coals. I read the sign hanging from the tarpaulin.

Genius. This can be the only time I've seen Dan so doggedly rooted to one spot. He's the human dynamo firing up the pedal-powered sound system. Maybe if

I'd had the nous to bring a lightweight exercise bike out clubbing with us he wouldn't have gone walkabout quite so often and our marriage would be in better shape.

I've seen it all. As we get closer I can hear ska-tinged dub step bouncing out of the tinny battered speakers propped up at either side of the awning. Dan's head is facing downwards, and he's pedalling determinedly. His Aviators are gone, replaced by some cheap-looking black plastic wrap-arounds and the lines fanning out from behind them to the side of his head are even more pronounced than normal. The grey marl-effect T-shirt he's got on is soaked and stuck to his back, but despite the primal physical efforts being made by his body, there's something robotic about him, something shell-like and empty. The sense of absence is compounded when I call his name, two, three times and there's no response, no sign of recognition whatsoever.

Amita has led me to the DIY Circle. Compared to the rest of the Lost Weekend, it is essentially a field where the main sound system is encased in an articulated lorry surrounded by a few small tents and a battalion of decommissioned ambulances and military vehicles. It's like the land that corporate sponsorship forgot. Without all the marketing clutter and in spite of T-shirts bearing a crippling fusion of psychedelic and pagan graphics, there's a sparseness, a weird visual quietness.

I've only ever been here once before, in the early nineties when there was all the hoo-ha about the week-long illegal rave at Castle Morton and the Criminal Justice Act. There was a brief moment in pop culture when crusties were relevant – living in trees and underground camps to stop roads being built, putting on illegal parties in the name of freedom. There was even one on *Coronation Street*. I was curious to see what today's dropouts were up to.

Not much has changed: the bleepy techno from the main sound system is as annoying as ever and there are still lots of stroppy girls with Mohawks, purple cropped tops and stripy tights. Even in this heat.

The mid-afternoon sun is hidden though, for the first time in days, by clouds, and the air is humid. Like the rest of the rinsed-out festival site, by Sunday afternoon, the DIY Circle is filthy. Plastic cups flattened into crude stars, squashed water bottles, flyers, half-eaten burgers, glow sticks and cardboard credit cards bearing information about the Samaritans, STD clinics and Eat Natural muesli bars are strewn across the trodden-down, worn-out grass. Thick green industrial sacks clipped to fences overflow. Piles and piles of rubbish surround them.

The veins on the side of Dan's head are bulging. He looks jaundiced.

'Hello, is anyone in there?' I tap the side of his head

with my index finger. His skin is cold but damp; his nose is covered with pregnant blackheads. 'Dan. It's time to go home.'

Still no response. Just a stubborn, soulless series of machinations. I've seen him in some states but never with so much spirit removed. I bend down onto my knees, see if my movement can engage him. Again nothing. He just keeps pedalling; the wheels keep on turning and the music keeps on coming.

I look back at Am who pulls a 'What are you going to do now?' face at me and then I spot Gary, without his leather jacket for once, propped up against a big plastic barrel. Kind of thing you'd see in a garden centre. He's out for the count. Eyes closed, head slouched, chin doubled up on his chest.

I stumble as I stand back up again and lunge at Amita in an effort not to fall over. 'Maybe it's better to leave him,' I say, thinking surely no one could suspect such a pathetic specimen of being public enemy number one, of putting an assistant from the hospitality tent on a ventilator. 'He'll sleep it off eventually with blow-job lips over there.'

I throw my thumb back in the direction of Gary but don't believe what I'm trying to convince Am of. She doesn't get the blow-job reference and I'm not in the mood to start retelling the story. She shuffles around a little bit, uncomfortable. 'Don't you think he looks ill?'

Yeah, sick in the head, I think, but, obliged to give it one last go, I step back over to the bike and give Dan's shoulder a shake. This time he shrugs it off. One more time. 'Dan, it's me. Come on. Stop that for a minute.'

I watch his dry, pale, scurvy lips move slightly. He mouths 'Fuck you'.

Incensed and without thinking, I grab a bottle of water out of Am's hand and chuck it over my husband. A couple of the girls nearby stop dancing to gawp. Dan pedals even faster and the music gets louder.

I'm not having this. 'You fucking ungrateful cunt,' I scream at the top of my voice and pour the rest of the water down inside his shades.

Finally he straightens up, removes the glasses, wipes his eyes. His legs are still pounding up and down. Breathless, he starts shrieking at me, like a lunatic: 'Get out of my fucking face – ' Dan's voice is trembling with anger – 'I'll fucking kill you.' The behaviour of the man in front of me, pedalling a stationary bicycle, is so surreal that it doesn't scare me.

His eyes are like something from a B-movie, wild with intensity but almost comedic with cartoon craziness. I think about the eyes in *Who Framed Roger Rabbit*.

If it weren't so sad, if it wasn't my husband, it would be ridiculous. Am starts to drag me away but I'm rooted to the spot as Dan's eyes start rolling and he keels over, off the bike, the pedals still spinning.

It's only when the music finally drones and drags to a halt that the last person stops dancing.

Thirty-one

Dark red blood seeps from a wound on Dan's temple. A sparrow-like female medic cleans it away with an antiseptic wipe and gives it a spray with an alcohol solution. The cut is not as bad as it looks. He bashed the side of his head on one of the bike pedals after he'd slumped off it onto the ground.

Coming to with blood dripping into his eyes has panicked him but Dan is infinitely more lucid and receptive than he was before, albeit with a cold sweat and goose bumps. I stroke his arm and listen carefully to the tiny, mousy middle-aged lady.

'Now then, Dan, I'm just going to put a dressing on that cut and I think that should be it.' She sounds weary having stayed up all night patching up drug casualties and drunks who have fallen on their heads. She sounds tired of telling people this weekend that it's time to throw in the towel. Then she says to me: 'If it starts bleeding heavily he'll need to go to A & E. Make sure he drinks lots of water. No more alcohol or anything else.' Now back at Dan: 'Your wife thought you'd had a heart attack and to be perfectly frank it's a miracle you haven't. Just a case of severe dehydration. Think yourself lucky.'

Dan carries on staring down at the ground like a schoolboy being chided by a teacher. I really did think he'd had a heart attack and it was terrifying, especially as I've started to hear more and more stories of men I know in their thirties having heart problems.

Neon's old art director Owen, aged thirty-four, had woken up with stabbing chest pains after a monumental bender. The place was in darkness and it dawned on him, amid the terror of crippling chest pains, that he had no idea where he actually was. So when he managed to crawl to a phone to dial 999, he couldn't give the address of the stranger's place he'd eventually finished up partying at. Instead, he was saved by the fact he'd used a landline that could be traced by the emergency services to the unfamiliar flat he'd almost died in.

The ashen tinge Owen had to his skin, the last time I saw him – after the heart attack – was similar to the greyness of Dan's right now. It must be at least a year ago. Someone said he's back at his parents' in Cheam, thinking of applying to a landscape gardening course in Norwich.

Now that I can see Dan's going to be OK though, I cool down. I've been suckered into another protracted painful episode of pseudo-rehabilitation for my husband. I genuinely care about the dangerous state of his health but I'm irked at my overall stupidity at getting drawn in this far with a man who clearly doesn't give himself the same level of concern.

'It'll be OK,' I say bossily. 'I've come to take him home.'

Am has been standing behind me the whole time and puts a hand on my shoulder, giving it a firm shake of support. I still utterly despise Dan though. I pity the state of this man, head bandaged, slumped on the floor next to me, and I want absolutely nothing more to do with him, but, in spite of everything, the right thing to do is get him home and tidy him up before pushing him back out into the world to face the music. Then he can fuck right off. If he really wants a heart attack, he can do it on his own.

I give a reassuring, responsible smile to the medic and put a bottle of water to Dan's lips while she packs her bag and then pulls herself to her feet.

A girl with a tiny pink ponytail that shoots right up off the top of her head is on the saddle of the bike now and the music winds back up again. Dan looks at me properly for the first time, cagily. This time I look away, to the girl on the bike's bare feet moulded into the pedals as they go round and round, and lift the tips of my fingers out of the long dark hair on his forearms.

The minute the medic is out of earshot he says, 'I'm not coming.'

I carry on watching the girl on the bike's chipped purple-varnished toenails make circles. 'You can't stay here, Dan.'

A man with rotten teeth and a matted ponytail bends in front of Dan. 'You all right now? Gotta keep the party alive, man.' He pats Dan on his head, gets back up and starts prancing around again. Where on earth do these people come from? What is wrong with everybody?

'I'm not coming,' he says again. I pass him some more water and he gives a tiny, reluctant smile of thanks.

'You can't hang out here any more, can you? Just because the drugs didn't kill you, don't think this fucking awful music won't.' The ponytailed girl on the bike has switched the music from the bouncy dub step Dan was throwing out of the sound system to deep, agonisingly awful, cranked-up techno.

'Where are your bags? Shall I get Tom to bring them over?'

He sighs. 'You're not listening to me.'

All I want to do is leave and get on the road. On my own preferably, but part of me is resigned to one more act of wifely duty. 'Look, if we get home tonight, you can get your head down and then get a plan together tomorrow. The police aren't going to stop looking for you. How many times do I have to say it?'

Emptily, Dan replies, 'Get off my case, Louisa . . . stop trying to control every fucking move I make. The Old Bill are my problem.'

'But if you come home now, get it together, you'll be in much better shape to go and talk to them.'

'Louisa, this isn't about the police. I'm not stupid. I know I'm in the shit and I'm going to deal with it. Just not today.' Dan looks at me, suddenly, with the most kindness he's shown me in weeks. 'I'm not coming back with you because I don't want to be with you any more. It's over.' He shuffles around awkwardly. 'Whether all this had happened or not.'

After pleading with Dan to come home and cut his losses on more occasions than I could ever remember, the perversity of begging him to now, when I really don't want him to, is not lost on me. But I still can't believe what I'm hearing. He's telling me that he's leaving. How the hell did he get to dumping me before I got to dumping him? Dan's on his arse with clumps of blood sticking out of his eyebrows after falling off that ridiculous bike and he's giving me the heave-ho. How did it happen that the biggest waster here got to give me my marching orders?

Our warped version of reality carries on playing out, only now I'm on the outside looking in. Today it's obvious that Dan pulls further in the other direction, with every single appeal I make. I wonder whether using reverse psychology in the past would have made a difference in the long run, but the dried clumps of blood also collecting in his ears remind me to get a grip. He's completely out of control, but increasingly reacting against me has given him, and me, the twisted sense that he's got some.

I've been given the golden ticket but my first reaction is to feel completely and utterly gutted, knocked for six, until the shock begins to dissolve and I remember that this, being set free, is what I actually want. I'm conscious not to show any shift in perspective. If he wants to leave me, let him.

We sit in silence, while the party carries on around us. Him ashen, ruined and wounded, me washed out, exhausted, with greasy hair and dirty knees. Through a gap in the dancing legs surrounding us I can see Gary, still out for a count and propped up against the barrel, his nose running, all watery.

'What are you going to do?' I ask quietly.

'I'm going back up to the farm. It goes through till tomorrow. I know I'm going to get stuck in the can for twatting that kid. Might as well go out with a bang.'

It wasn't what I meant. I was asking Dan where he was going to stay, who he was going to live with. In spite of everything he still can't see beyond his own nose.

'Well, there isn't really anything I can say, is there? You've made up your mind.' I start to cry, then weep into my hands. Sadness, disappointment, relief, exhaustion, nausea, emptiness and lightness pulling me upwards. All at once. It's overwhelming. I can finally get away.

Dan reads it far too simply, he doesn't have the capacity to deal with the complexity of any real emotion, and puts his arm around me. 'Babes, you'll be fine. It's just the way things have to be. I'm sorry but it's over.'

I carry on sobbing and he edges away. 'I can't talk about this any more ... Make sure you calm down before you leave. I'll worry about you in that car otherwise.'

Fucking cheek, I think to myself. Dan staggers to his feet, says goodbye and is gone.

Amita, who's been keeping her distance while all this has been going on, pulls me up to my feet, cradles my face with her long, bony fingers and looks into my eyes. 'Come on, let's get you out of this hole.'

I sway around, delirious with the onslaught of emotions running through me.

'I'm fine, honestly.' It's true: I'm done in by everything,

but I'm going to be fine. I'll be back in a little while. I just need some time on my own.'

One thing Am understands more than anyone is being dumped. She kisses my forehead and leaves me to swim in my thoughts.

Thirty-two

The mobile police unit is essentially a huge van covered in blue-and-yellow graphics that opens up from the side with a big awning. Switch the logos and it's not dissimilar to a jumbo fish-and-chip van. It's the cleanest place on-site.

Two girls – they sound like they're Spanish – have been with the WPC at what is for all intents and purposes the front desk for ages, giving details of everything that's been stolen from their tent. Camera, stereo, passports.

I have never felt so alone. Everything about me – my skin, my hair, the inside of my throat – is dry, withered. My cuticles are thick and crusty. I remind myself of Dan lying on the floor with his head bleeding. This is the only way to stop the rot.

Eventually, down in the mouth but with a reasonable-size claim on their travel insurance secured, the girls slouch away from the counter. 'Good morning, madam. What can I do for you?'

My voice is wobbly. I explain to the officer, very quietly, I was here yesterday with PC Marden to answer some questions about a fight on Friday night. 'I've started to remember a lot more.'

The WPC becomes more animated and shuffles about but remains professionally monotone. 'And you are?'

'Louisa Parker. I'm married to Dan Taylor, the guy you're looking for.'

The interview room is a partitioned section to the rear of the van. I'm offered some water and I sit down on the same black vinyl seat I'd spent a couple of hours in yesterday. This time I rest on the edge of the seat, look at my knees, and patiently wait for the officer with me to open the right file on his laptop. I dip my fingers into the water and pat my eyes and smooth around the contours of my face.

'So, Mrs Taylor, what's happening? I understand you have some more information relating to the assault of David Lester?'

The officer sounds weary, and abrupt with it. He's not accusatory, though, as had been the tone yesterday. I'm sure they've taken no end of statements from others who saw the fight and were more forthcoming than I had been, brutally descriptive and uninhibited in their depiction of what they saw. The man whose socks dry next to mine on the radiator is already nailed a hundred times over. I give my account, faithfully this time, anyway.

I very deliberately relay, for instance, how Dan covered his top teeth with his bottom lip when he headbutted David on his right temple and the exact direction in which Dan ran afterwards. I was a bit drunk when it happened and I've been in shock, I think, I say, but it's all come back to me. I raise my eyebrows and shake my head. I can't defend my husband, I say. I imagine there's a chance I'll have to repeat and elaborate it all in court at some point too.

I ask how David Lester is bearing up. Slight improvement, apparently.

The walk over here, from the DIY Circle, across the whole site more or less, had taken fifteen minutes. It was a reluctant, slow admission of failure in many senses. To have chosen another path would have represented an even bigger one in the long run.

'I've just heard he's still here, bloody idiot, and I'm pretty sure where you'll find him,' I say, my face ugly and twisted, my mouth suddenly full of saliva. The policeman offers me no comfort. Why would he? I'm just another in a long line of stupid women propping up useless men.

He remains blank-faced and I dribble out Dan's whereabouts. He steps out of the room for a moment and I hear a radio crackle as another officer talks into it. It's done. My jaw begins to relax, my eyebrows soften and I'm left with an uncomfortable, surreal expansiveness in my head that flows down across my chest. There's no going back. I sign my statement and walk back outside. Numb.

Thirty-three

Leaving the door wide open to get rid of the smell of flat beer, I gather the rubbish – the crushed-up fag packets and empty Stella cans – that covers the passenger-seat footwell of my car and walk over to the outer edge of the car park to bin it all.

Walking back again towards the car, I'm reminded of arriving here a couple of days ago. I watch people packing rucksacks, party hats and cool boxes into their boots, sedated by the onset of the Sunday-night blues, and begin to wonder what kind of lives they might be off home to. It's half past six, a couple of hours later than I'd hoped to head off at, but I should still just about get back to the flat without falling asleep at the wheel.

I twist the knob on the stereo down before I turn the keys in the ignition to get the engine running and then poke around in the glove compartment until I find the CD I'm looking for, a soft meandering instrumental soundtrack to a full-length *Charlie Brown* movie. It's calming, comforting and unobtrusive, yet still enough to help carry me along the road back home with a gentle push.

It starts plinky-plonkying away and I do a last-minute check through my bag and purse so that I have everything I'll need for the next few hours to hand. I'm not used to driving such long distances on my own, especially on the motorway.

I find my wedding ring in the zip pocket of my bag and put it in the little plastic well in between the handbrake and the gearstick, along with half a dozen one- and two-pence pieces. It's silly, I don't know what I should do with it and, for a tiny piece of platinum, it feels like it's occupying a hugely disproportionate amount of space in the VW, prompting thoughts that I'd rather leave dormant until next week.

Like, it's not just the case of dividing our stuff up and packing bags. Dan and I are going to get divorced. There's no point in separating; it's not like there's anything to salvage and I have an overriding feeling of needing to be legally severed from him as quickly as possible.

Where do you begin with all that? How am I going

to pay for a lawyer? I don't even know how to start looking for one.

I crunch into reverse and snarl at myself for getting my knickers in a twist over it already. I might not have much myself but I've virtually bankrolled him since we met. Enough, I say, aloud. I tip my ear to one side, inviting the calmness of the music to take up residence in my brain instead of all the other nonsense.

The clapped-out VW bumps along the uneven tracks worn into the grass by days of cars toing and froing, gently jolting me away from the noise and the carnage of the festival. Almost all the other cars slowly worming their way along towards the exit are steered by yawning, slouching, sunburnt drivers and packed with passengers, shades on, staring out of wound-down windows into the early-evening sunshine that's breaking through.

My car's suspension takes a hammering and then it's the clutch as we inch up a steep, chalky incline towards the gates. A couple of teenage boys with shaggy indie-boy hair and skinny jeans stand in the dust, next to the line of cars, bags by their feet, thumbs out. I'm forced to stop, still, right next to them and they stare into my empty car while I hide behind my sunglasses and pull my arm in from the open window. They ask if I'm heading towards London but I give them the brush-off and carry on looking out of the dirty windscreen. I release the handbrake and nudge forward a few metres. One of them calls me a miserable bitch. I crack a smile. Cheeky little shits. 'It's better than being a stupid one,' I shout out of the window back at them.

The sensation at the top of the slope, the feeling of the car's tyres against proper tarmac, takes me by surprise and I pull off with a burst of the same nervousness and excitement that you get when you roll off a cross-Channel ferry, into a new country where they drive on the other side of the road. At the same time as a couple of stray tears leak out, I blow a big sigh, and poke my fingers into my greasy hair, trying to get some of the air that's coming through the window to circulate through it. It still smells of stale beer and fags inside. You can do this, Louisa, I tell myself and I'm surprised that I feel confident. I am going to deal with whatever's coming my way over the next few months.

The car will need a bit of external assistance though if we're going to get back to London any time this week. The minute I move up out of third gear as the narrow, winding country roads surrounding the festival site open up and the traffic begins to stretch out, the petrol light pings on. Balls, I've got about fifteen, maybe twenty quid left. Please let it be enough to get me home.

The petrol station just off the roundabout that filters onto the motorway is jammed with cars and SUVs. It's packed with wistful weekending families, sad to say goodbye to the countryside, and washed-out festivalgoers, glum about the inevitable: pulling out a chair and switching on a computer tomorrow morning.

I wait in the queue, looking down at my grimy fingernails as I rest the back of my hands on the steering wheel. The air is thick with fumes and the sound of the pumps droning away, interspersed with engines stopping and starting. How on earth did I get to thinking that I was any different to anyone else? No one wants the party to end but sometimes it has to.

Eventually, after sliding forward a few feet a time for ten minutes, it's my turn. I have no idea how many miles my car does to the gallon. Why would I? The digits on the pump have only ever been boring details that mean nothing to me. Until now, the car's either got some petrol in it, or it hasn't. I normally squeeze a fiver's worth onto one credit card or the other, along with ten Marlboro Menthols, and get from A to B by the skin of my teeth.

Tonight, I stick fifteen quid in and hope for the best, but soon, I tell myself, the new improved me might even become one of those people who stands and waits for the pump to jolt to a halt, with the tank full right up.

Despite having been so impatient to leave earlier, I find myself lingering in the aisles of the forecourt shop, browsing the toiletries section, before handing over my cash. It's only the chorus of horns beeping in the queue outside that pushes me up to the counter and back out to the car again.

I jump in, start up the engine and pull off, over into a parking space just at the front of the shop where I try to stuff my receipt into my purse but it won't close properly. The top of it gets caught in the zip and I'm forced to empty all the contents onto the passenger seat and start again.

Only then do I admit to myself the real reason behind my reluctance to get a move on and, finally, zoom away up the motorway. The small lilac compliments slip, also in my purse, with Matt's number on, has been tugging away at me, even more doggedly than my abandoned wedding ring. I press both middle fingers into my eyebrows, trying to give my tired eyes some more focus, stare down at the number and examine the handwriting. Even if I had any juice in my phone there's no way I've got the balls to dial it. He probably wouldn't even pick up anyway after the mix-up with Amita earlier. Instead I decide to do something even more rash. I reverse out of the parking bay and drive back onto the roundabout where I sail past the blue sign for the M4 and take the turn-off towards the village where Matt's staying.

Thirty-four

The young guy on reception calls up to Matt's room. I feel like turning round and sprinting back out the door. I'm out of my mind.

'Fine, sir, I'll send her up.'

I feel sick. What if I read it all completely wrong and he was just being decent watching out for me last night?

'Miss, room number 8. Up the staircase to your left and it's at the very end.'

This is such a ridiculous thing to do. Why didn't I just carry on up the M4?

Holmwood House isn't a yokel, local sixty quid a night B & B with aggressive floral carpets, but an incredibly well-thought-out, smart, bijou hotel for savvy, urban professionals. Traditional stone on the outside and subtly, stealthily modern on the inside. The neutral

293

walls and wooden floors say low-key, casual sophistication. Against such a carefully put-together backdrop I must look like a right mess.

When I reach the top of the stairs I check the inside corners of both eyes for deposits of mascara that might have collected there. Matt is standing in the open doorway at the end of the corridor. Now I really do want to run.

'Well, well, didn't expect to see you,' he says. He genuinely looks quite pleased to see me but surprised and curious as to why I've appeared on his doorstep. 'Everything OK?' Good question. I ignore it. 'Hello.' I'm embarrassed at my intrusion and outwardly cringe as I walk up to the door.

'How did you know to come here?'

I bite my lip and hold up the comp slip. 'I know it's probably a bit weird, me just turning up . . .'

He steps aside. 'Don't be daft. Come in.'

Inside, the room is a mix of white linen, dark wooden furniture and wooden floorboards. There's a moss-green mohair throw at the end of the bed, a Bang & Olufsen TV in the corner and a small cream daybed covered in clothes. He's got some country music on with a folky American guy mumbling away over the top of it.

Matt shuts the door and leans against a low sideboard. He's wearing baggy, well-worn, patched-up jeans that I can see are vintage Levi's, a plain white T-shirt and some purple Vans. His stubble has pushed through into a nearly beard. He looks good.

'I just wanted to say thanks, for last night.' I stand in the middle of the room, fiddling with my hands. In my awkwardness, I consider saying that I've got Lottie's sweatshirt in the car and wanted to make sure she got it back but I don't. I say nothing instead.

'Louisa, you're making me uncomfortable. Sit down.'

'I'm sorry. Maybe I shouldn't have come over.'

Matt starts laughing. 'Sit down, will you? I'm glad you stopped by. I've got tomorrow off and everyone else has already gone home. I haven't got any plans tonight. It was just Billy No Mates, room service and the TV till you turned up.'

I perch on the edge of the bed and remember him telling me how he normally liked to spend the weekend alone.

'I don't want to screw up your evening, but so much happened this weekend and I'm really grateful you stepped in like you did.'

He looks coy. 'Just being a good citizen. As long as everything's OK now?'

It will be, I tell him, determinedly. I want him to understand that I'm not about to slip back down the hole he helped wrench me out of any time soon. That I appreciate him sticking it out with me last night, more than he can ever imagine. I set things straight, explain what's happened with Dan, Alexa and, more positively, with Dad.

'Blimey, it really all kicked off, didn't it? Still, better to get it all over and done with in one big hit, hey?' I find myself hoping his casualness is because he's pleased to hear that I've split from Dan and not just because he has a much healthier sense of perspective on life than I do.

'Maybe,' I say, 'but from now on, I want life to be much quieter. I mean, look at me . . .' I pull at my hair, my face, my dress and laugh at the sorry state I'm in.

'Look, I tell you what – ' Matt goes into practical mode – 'let me run you a bath. Maybe we can grab some food afterwards.'

He doesn't give me time to agree or disagree, but heads into the bathroom and I follow, where I watch the piping-hot water rise in the white enamel bath. Steam begins to fill the room. He squirts in some Kiehl's cucumber soap and puts it back into his smart brown leather toiletries bag.

'Everything's going to be OK.' He pauses and looks at me. 'I told you before. You're a smart girl.' He kisses me lightly on the cheek. 'Take as long as you want.'

Matt closes the door and I peel my clothes off. Naked, I stand by the sink, examining my oversized face in the shaving mirror for a minute or so, and then step into the water.

Thanks

First and foremost to Cathryn Summerhayes and Eugenie Furniss at William Morris Endeavor, Rowan Yapp at Vintage and Barney Calman, for their brilliant advice, tough love and precious time. Big thanks also to Marius W Hansen, Rana Reeves, Bob Page, Jenny Owen, Amie Wallace and Sacha Lynch-Robinson for their various skills, wise words and generous support.

I'm totally indebted to a very long list of amazing friends and family who have helped make this book happen, especially my mum, a constant inspiration, and my late father, who gave me the confidence to put pen to paper for a living in the first place. Last but not least, Archie and Wilma, thank you my darlings for not banging on the door when I'm writing.